LONG WALK

HOME

JOHN L. LANSDALE

BookVoice Publishing 2020

Long Walk Home Copyright © 2018
by John L. Lansdale
All rights reserved.

Cover illustration Copyright © 2014
All rights reserved.

The NIEA name and logo are the registered trademarks of National Indie Excellence Awards.

First BookVoice Paperback Edition © 2020

ISBN
978-1-949381-19-1 Paperback
978-0-9990361-6-7 Hardcover
978-0-9990361-7-4 eBook

BookVoice Publishing
PO Box 1528
Chandler, TX 75758
www.bookvoicepublishing.com

THE MECANA FILES by John L. Lansdale

#1 – Horse of a Different Color
#2 – When the Night Bird Sings
#3 – Twisted Justice
#4 – The Box

Other Titles by John L. Lansdale

Zombie Gold
Slow Bullet
Long Walk Home
Kissing the Devil
The Last Good Day
Broken Moon
Shadows West (with Joe R. Lansdale)
Hell's Bounty (with Joe R. Lansdale)
Boy and Hog
Boy and Hog Return
Emergency Christmas
Tales from the Crypt
That Hellbound Train
Yours Truly, Jack the Ripper
Shadow Warrior
Justin Case

What Others are Saying about John L. Lansdale

"*Long Walk Home* really touched and gripped me. A great bitter-sweet story of light and shadow about growing up in a time gone by. I loved it." – Joe R. Lansdale

A "page-turner...Lansdale effectively delays revealing the novel's big secret until the end. Those who like their thrillers with a heavy dose of violent action will be satisfied."
– *Publishers Weekly* review of **Slow Bullet**

"This is an entertaining, science fiction-historical-horror blend with resourceful protagonists and a solid cast of secondary characters." – *Booklist* review of **Zombie Gold**

"The author's innate ability to spin a complex tale painted with vivid characters and intense suspense provides readers with a well-paced book that they may find difficult to set down...a worthwhile suspenseful ride."
– *Amazing Stories* review of **Horse of a Different Color**

"A straight-ahead thriller...it's about action, and there's plenty of that. Check it out."
– *Bill Crider's Pop Culture Magazine* review of **Slow Bullet**

"Has something for everyone... It's exciting, entertaining and educational. A fun ride."
– TV personality Joan Hallmark review of **Zombie Gold**

"Something unique and comfortable and difficult to put down. Highly recommended."
– *Cemetery Dance* review of **Hell's Bounty**

"True to Lansdale tradition, John L. Lansdale has compiled a piece of work that should appeal to a wide range of readers."
– *Amazing Stories* review of **Zombie Gold**

*In joyful memory of
Buddy and O'Reta Lansdale.
The best parents a boy could have.
They did it with love.*

"An old young man will be a young old man."
Benjamin Franklin

PART ONE
WHAT'S IN A NAME

(1)

I had never seen Beau in a suit and tie before. I was glad I got a chance to say goodbye. In my memory I could see him running like the wind through Mama's pasture on those hot summer days in 1944 when we were ten. My grandma used to say it was a shame the good Lord didn't put that speed in his head instead of his feet.

As I sat there, waiting for the funeral service to start, the memories of that last summer on the farm were as clear as if it happened yesterday.

It was a life-changing time for all of us in Angel Point, Mississippi, though it started out like any other.

I had my chores, but I didn't have to go to school, do homework, wear shoes or, best of all, help Beau Sterling with his arithmetic.

Almost everyone old enough was off fighting Germans in the war. Seemed everyone else worked at the canning factory or on one of the farms around Angel Point. It was where General Sherman crossed on his way to Vicksburg during the Civil War.

Not much ever changed until the summer of 1944, when everything changed forever.

Out of the corner of my eye I saw a pretty young lady with a small boy walk up beside me.

"Mr. O'Rourke?" she said as I stood up.

"Yes ma'am," I said.

"Thought so. I saw your name on the guest list," she said. "My name's Helen Massy. My grandpa Beau thought a lot of you. I know it was difficult getting to Alaska in this weather. Thank you for coming."

"We were best friends as boys," I said.

"It was my grandpa's suggestion I name my boy Trenton after you," she said. "Maybe we can talk more after the funeral?"

"I would enjoy that," I said and patted little Trenton on the shoulder. Helen nodded and led Trenton back to their seats.

I sat back down in the pew and noticed from the open casket Beau had his pilot wings pinned on. Every now and then someone would walk by and touch or rub the wings. With the delay in the funeral from waiting for more guests to arrive, the wings might not be on his chest by the time the funeral started.

Beau wasn't his real name but they called him that because his sister came along five years before he did. Mr. Sterling's name was Henry and they weren't sure they would have a boy. He wanted a junior, so they named the girl Henrietta and called her Henry. When Beau was born, Mr. Sterling still wanted a junior, so Beau was named Henry Alexander Sterling Jr. Three Henrys was a bit much, so his sister started calling him Beau, short for brother, and that's how Beau got his name.

The deeper I went into my memories the more I thought about my own family.

They called my father Buzz because he once worked in a saw mill. My mother's name was Elizabeth and they called her Liz. She died when I was five from some kind of heart problem that Doc Crawford said she was born with. Aunt Sara Beth was the only one without a nickname. My mother and Aunt Sara Beth were raised by their grandmother. Their mom and dad were killed in a bus wreck when mother and Aunt Sara Beth were little. I called my only grandparent Mama. She liked Mama better than grandma because that's what my daddy and uncle called her.

My Uncle Earl was away fighting Germans somewhere. He didn't have a nickname now but Mama said when he was little everyone called him Squirrel because he was always trying to make people laugh.

A man wearing a bearskin coat walked by me toward the casket and broke my train of thought with a whiff of his coat. Most of the people at the funeral were wearing heavy fur coats. The only way to and from town this far north was by air.

As I looked around the pews at the rest of the crowd, the young lady I met earlier shrugged her shoulders to indicate we were still waiting and smiled. I lip synced the words "No problem." She nodded and smiled again and I returned to my memories to wait.

(2)

The next thing I thought of was my dad picking cotton in the Delta and Mama and me working with a sharecropper to save what we had left on the farm. Nate the sharecropper was an old black man who lived down in the river land area. He was a muscular man with short, kinky gray hair and a cloudy right eye he said got caught on a fish hook when he was seven. He said he could see shadows out of it but that was all. He was what whites referred to as high yellow. He probably had some white blood in him somewhere along the way. Mama said he showed up in Angel Point about the time I was born, after killing a white man in a prize fight down in New Orleans. Unusual for a one-eyed man.

Most of the colored worked as share croppers or at the canning factory. Mama told me it was dangerous down there in the river land for a white boy and to never go by myself.

A black doctor named Oswald Stevens moved down from New Jersey in June of '44 because old Doc Crawford would only treat whites. It was rumored Doctor Stevens came to Angel Point because he got caught in Newark with another man's wife and her husband was going to kill him.

Doc Crawford said he didn't have anything against colored but he trained to be a white doctor and that was the way he was going to keep it. He came to the school once and gave a talk about himself. Everyone in town was pretty proud of him. He said he was born and raised in Angel Point, went off to college and medical school to take care of his own. He had been in World War I. He tried to volunteer for this one but he was too old. He was kind of skinny, with sky blue eyes and thin gray hair. He wore a white starched shirt and khakis every day like some people wear a uniform. A group of blacks from Vicksburg found out about him not treating them right and said they were going to have the medical board take his license away for unethical conduct, but they never did. White folks owned all the businesses and made it clear that if they did, nobody in town would have a job for them and they couldn't buy anything at the stores.

Mama thought Doc Crawford was dead wrong.

Nate worked the crops every day except Sunday. We rode to church with the Sterlings every Sunday. Uncle Earl had left his Ford coupe at home, but Mama couldn't drive and had no plans to learn. She said driving a motor car was un-lady-like and should be left to men.

On Saturdays, Mama would let me go to town with Nate to go to the movies if I had done my chores. So I gathered the eggs, wrung a chicken's neck for supper and cleaned the rain barrel while Nate hitched up Homer the mule and loaded the wagon.

.I finished my chores and went in to get an okay from Mama to go to town.

"If it's alright for me to go with Nate, I need my milk bottles," I said.

"You did good," Mama said. "They in the kitchen. I'll get them."

It took two hours to go the four miles to town. Homer was never in any hurry and Nate said he was old and let him take his time. Sometimes Nate would fall asleep and Homer would go right on tugging the wagon to town on the dirt road with white sand along the sides that was always scalding hot from the summer sun.

We could smell the blackberries and peaches in the fields as we rode along but Nate wouldn't let me go get any because they belonged to someone else.

"You never take anything that's not yours," he said.

I would get bored moving so slow, get off the wagon and run alongside like I was a desperado about to rob a stage and take the gold. My bare feet would get hot in the sand and I would have to run to the shade to cool them off every little bit.

We sold the vegetables in the wagon yard in town with all the other farmers. Sometime as many as twenty wagons would be lined up, selling everything from fruit and vegetables to mules, horses, cattle and whatever someone wanted to get rid of.

We would be through at the wagon yard by one or two in the afternoon. Nate would give me Mama's share. I would put the money in my pocket tied to a lead fishing weight to keep from losing it. Nate and Homer would go on home.

I would stash the two milk bottles Mama gave me for picture show money in my secret hiding place at the wagon yard and run the streets of Angel Point, first checking out the motor airplane hanging in the mercantile store's window to see if it was still there. They wanted twenty-five dollars for it. Daddy said he didn't have the money to buy it, but maybe he could get it for Christmas. I was sure it would be gone by then.

Mr. Grayson would always let me hold the plane when I came in.

"Well, Tee, I hope you get that airplane. It's the best toy I've got," Grayson said.

23

"Daddy said he may can get it for Christmas if you don't sell it. But that's a long time off," I said.

"Yeah," Mr. Grayson said. "Someone comes in to buy it, I got to let it go for the money I have tied up in it. Your Daddy still picking cotton in the delta?"

"Yes sir. See you later," I said.

"Tell him to come by and see me when he comes home."

"I will. Bye, Mr. Grayson."

My next stop was the farm supply store to see the new animals. They usually got a new batch in every week. They had goats, pigs, rabbits, chickens and sometimes people would bring their puppies and kittens in to sell or give away. One time I brought a puppy home, but Mama made me take it back.

Mr. Simpson was putting some pups in a cage when I came in.

"Hi, Tee," he said. "Your grandma going to let you have a pup?"

"No, just looking," I said and went on to the candy factory.

A bunch of kids were watching them make peppermint candy sticks through the big glass window at the candy factory when I got there and the sugar smell was drifting outside, making us all hungry. A woman wearing a white apron came out and gave us all a free peppermint stick.

Angel Point was a small town but I liked it. We kind of had one of everything; like a hardware store, picture show, café, drug store, grocery, mercantile store and a bank. I had never been in the bank. Mama said you couldn't trust banks. She said Grandpa lost all their money when the banks failed in '29. Now she kept her money in a fruit jar under her bed.

If I had time before the next picture show started I would go down to the square and look at the two old covered wagons with stuffed-cotton people and horses. One of those stuffed men was supposed to be my grandpa's grandpa and they had a sign forbidding smoking nearby. Since most men did, they would sometimes light up next to the stuffed people in protest.

Mama said Grandpa O'Rourke's family was one of the first to come to Angel Point from Ireland, along with some Scottish relatives.

They had a statue of a Choctaw Indian Chief on the square. A sign said his name was Pushmataha. No one could pronounce his name, so everyone called him Push and rubbed his head for good luck until it was slap-dab smooth. According to our teachers, his tribe was here before the white man came. He befriended the settlers and helped them get through their first winter. The Indians called the place Spirit Point. The white settlers preferred angels to spirits and that's how the town got its name, or at least that's what they told us in school.

When I got tired of looking around I would fetch my milk bottles and sell them at Tucker's Grocery Store for a dime a piece. Mr. Tucker always had some big live catfish laying on a newspaper outside his store for sale on Saturday that you could smell a block away and I would stop and just watch them breathe for a few minutes before I went in the store. I felt kind of sorry for them. They were dying a slow death. There was nothing I could do, so I went on about my business. The catfish would be supper for someone in Angel Point that night anyway. Mr. Tucker's hired hand Willie Alcott would check the bottles to make sure they weren't cracked before he would give me my dimes. He banged one on the counter one time, broke it, and wouldn't give me my dime. He said it was an accident but I think he did it on purpose. Once in a while I would trade a milk bottle for some fish hooks, or sinkers for me and Beau to go fishing, or some batteries for my radio.

It cost a dime to get in the movie. I would spend the other dime on popcorn and a Coke if I didn't trade it away. If I wanted more money I would stand on the corner at the Rexall drug store and sing "One Dozen Roses" for people passing by. They would throw pennies on the side walk. Sometimes I would get nickels and dimes and make over a dollar. Mama didn't like for me to do that so I kept it to my-self.

After the movie I would make that long walk home stuffed with popcorn and candy. I would hide my stash un-der my bed when I got home, let Mama know I was back, eat supper to conceal my drug store singing and then be sick all night. The trade-off began to bother me so much I quit singing.

(3)

One Saturday I never got around to going to the movies because there were too many other things going on. When me and Nate got to town everyone was lined up on Main Street like there was going to be a parade, but we hadn't heard about any. Nate walked up to an old black man he knew and asked what was going on.

"The Army's bringing a load of German prisoners through town on their way to the prison camp in Vicksburg. If I had a gun I'd shoot me one," the old man said.

Nate didn't know what to say to that so he patted the old man on the shoulder and we moved on down the street. Like everyone else in town, we had never seen any real live Germans before, so we waited, too.

We were distracted for a little while by a fight that broke out outside the drug store, over who got to stand where, but a sheriff's deputy they called Sammy broke it up and hauled Tinker Bishop away to jail for having too much to drink. He smelled like sour grapes and made me sick to my stomach.

Willie brought a case of cold soda pop out of Tucker's store and hawked it down the street for a nickel to whoever wanted one. Nate bought us one and that helped my stomach so we lined up with everyone else, drinking soda pop and waiting on the Germans. About a half hour later we heard the roar of truck engines. Nate picked me up and sat me on his shoulder.

Rolling through town were ten trucks carrying German prisoners, with the letters POW on the side, and behind each of those trucks drove another with a machine gun pointed at the prisoners. People threw whatever they could find at the Germans, including the soda pop bottles. Some of the prisoners were bleeding as they disappeared out of town.

By the time the Germans were gone and we sold the vegetables I had missed Johnny Mack Brown and Sunset Carson, so I kept my dimes and went on home. I didn't say anything to Mama about the Germans. I told her I was saving my money. I didn't want to remind her of the war.

My Grandpa Wendon was in World War I but got sick and passed away before I was born, leaving Mama to fend for herself. She farmed and raised her two boys. He was a lot older than Mama, I think.

Mama was old now, maybe sixty. Her hands were callused and her face showed the years of working in the fields. She had a small scar under her chin where the cellar door caught her during a storm. Her long mixed red and gray hair hung past her waist, but no one ever saw it. She kept it tied in a bun all the time tucked under her bonnet. She would let it down every night before she went to bed and run a brush through it a hundred times. It was always a hundred times. Sometimes I would count the strokes to see if it was always a hundred. It was.

Mama came to Mississippi from Ireland when she was 14 to marry my grandpa. It was a family-arranged wedding by the O'Rourke and McBride families in Ireland. She had a wedding picture that sat on her bed table. She was a pretty fourteen-year-old girl with big blue eyes and bright red hair.

Grandpa was a big handsome man with green eyes, shoulder length brown hair and a black handlebar moustache. You could see the resemblance of him in Daddy, except for the long hair and mustache. Uncle Earl and I looked more like the McBrides, with red hair and blue eyes.

Mama never missed a Sunday going to church or saying her prayers at night. She always had on a white apron and wore it like it was a shield of armor. Nothing got past the apron. The first thing she would do before considering a solution to anything would be to wipe her hands on the apron. Daddy said it was just one of Mama's quirks. I didn't know what a quirk was and was afraid to ask.

My grandma was named Alma, but I had better not call her that. She said children don't call their elders by their first name. Daddy told me to do what Mama said, even if I didn't like it, because she was old and probably right about whatever it was anyway.

I liked being at Mama's. She was never mean to me and I got to do most of what I wanted in the summer time.

I heard the sound of someone walking in the church and it took me away from the memories again.

Two big men in their twenties wearing fur coats walked up to Mrs. Massy and spoke to her. She got up and whispered to the preacher and sat back down. He walked up to the podium and pushed the microphone to his mouth.

"Mrs. Massy said there's three more on the way who are going to be late because of the weather, maybe as much as two hours, and wants us to wait. But if anyone thinks they should leave there's no hard feelings."

A man and a woman got up and left but everyone else stayed. It crossed my mind to leave but I thought better of it and returned to the memories. It was an unbelievable time, that summer when I was ten.

(4)

Although I didn't know it then, that summer would be my last one at Mama's. Beau and I went fishing, hunted squirrels and played war almost every day. I was always the Captain. We had .22 single-shot Remingtons, and the rest of the kids only had Daisy air rifles. There was some discussion about that from the neighbors, especially the Cartwrights, who had two little girls. One of Mrs. Cartwright's girls, Emily, was in my class at school and Shirley was a year or two younger.

Every week or so, Mrs. Cartwright would go on a tear and start something with someone about boys being too young to have .22's and how afraid she was that we would shoot one of her little girls. They lived over a mile from us so I don't know how she thought that could happen. Plus, I wasn't allowed to hunt anywhere but on Mama's land. Mama said it didn't make any difference, Mrs. Cartwright was a natural born troublemaker, someone who got pleasure out of stirring up things. It gave her a purpose in life.

She was skinny, had dirty-looking brown hair, and long twig-like fingers that looked like they might snap off any minute. She had a wild eye that wouldn't always stay focused with the other one. Someone said it was caused from too many cousins marrying cousins. Her husband was also her first cousin. Mr. Cartwright was in the Navy and there was talk around town that she had found her a new favorite cousin.

Nevertheless, we got to keep the .22's and Mrs. Cartwright went right on complaining.

When I wasn't hunting or fishing I was helping Mama with the chores. She needed all the help she could get with my uncle away at war and my dad picking cotton. Mama had a red flag with a silver star on it in the window so people would know she had a son in the war. Daddy didn't have to go to war. He was what they called 4-F.

He lost the hearing in his left ear from the mumps when he was my age. Sheriff Charlie Bowman came by every once in a while and checked on us. I never knew why he wasn't drafted. He always had on his white ten-gallon cowboy hat, a badge and a pistol strapped around his waist. He was big enough to go bear hunting with a switch. I couldn't imagine what kind of situation he could get into that he would need the pistol. His cowboy boots made him look even bigger.

Mama said she wasn't worried. The good Lord would take care of her. And Nate was there every day except Sunday. Daddy said you could trust Nate because he was a man of his word. Besides, she kept a loaded double-barrel shotgun by her bed and knew how to use it.

(5)

The next Saturday when Nate and I went to town, he tied Homer under a shade tree and uncovered the vegetables. He didn't feel good so he let me do the bargaining. I had watched him enough to be pretty good at it. Nate said that if you always let the other guy make the first offer, you've got a starting point to make a profit.

Nate sat under the big umbrella he had over the wagon seat and dozed off and on. A couple of young black men wearing overalls and no shoes came up to the wagon and one pitched a quarter on the seat beside Nate, and picked up a bushel of beans. One of them was a little bigger than Nate and the other one tall and skinny.

Before I could say anything Nate spoke. "That's sixty five cents," he said.

"Looks like a quarter's worth to me," the big one said and turned to walk away with the beans.

"Nope, its sixty five cents if you want 'em," Nate said. "If you don't, put 'em back in the wagon."

"I gave you a quarter and that's all I'm goin' to give you, old man," the big one said.

Nate pushed his old straw hat back on his head and stood up on the wagon seat. "Boy, it's been a long day. I don't feel good, and I'm too old to fool with the likes of you. But if you don't put that basket down and get on your way, I'm goin' to have to kick your ass." Nate looked at me. "Excuse the language, Tee. Your grandma probably shouldn't know I said that."

I nodded that I understood and Nate climbed down from the wagon seat.

The skinny one moved behind Nate while the big one stood in front of him holding the basket.

"I really don't want any trouble over a bushel of beans," Nate said. "But I can't let you steal our property. Give me fifty cents and we call it a deal."

"Your property? It's that white boy's property," the big one said. "He's just using you like all the white folks do. You're probably not gettin' more than a dime a bushel anyway."

"He gets his share, I get mine. It's none of your business," Nate said.

"You'd rather bow down to that snot-nose white boy than help your own kind."

"Let him have them Nate, it's okay," I said.

"Can't do that, Tee. It's not right. If the boy said he needed help would be one thing, but to do what he's doin' is a whole different thing.

"For the last time, boy," Nate said, trying to hand back the quarter, "are you going to put that basket down or not?"

Several farmers had gathered around, waiting to see what was going to happen next.

I heard one of the farmers say, "I got a dollar on Nate if anybody wants it." No one said a word.

The tall skinny one charged Nate from behind. Nate wheeled around and landed a right square on the boy's jaw. I heard a pop and he went down like he was shot.

The big one sat the basket down and took a swing at Nate. Nate ducked and came up with an uppercut to the chin that lifted him clean off his feet. He fell to the ground on his back. Neither one moved.

"It's all over," Nate said, looking at the crowd that had gathered. He walked over to the big one and dropped the quarter on his chest. He picked up the basket and sat it back in the wagon, untied Homer, climbed up on the wagon seat, took down his umbrella and sat down.

"Tee, I think we call it a day. I don't feel too good and we about sold it all anyway. I will pay your grandma for what's left over. Here's your part for what we sold." He handed me the money. "You go on to the movies and be careful goin' home. I'll see you Monday." He picked up the reins, gave Homer a slight tap on the back as the mule slowly walked away pulling the wagon.

I wanted to say something to him about how quick he took care of those two guys, but I didn't know what to say. He was twice my father's age but I wondered if he could whip Daddy in a boxing ring.

Nate went home and I went to the movies. I didn't say anything to Mama about what happened in town. I figured Nate didn't want me to. He must be coming down with something. He looked awfully tired. I hoped he got better. We couldn't afford to lose Nate and didn't know anyone else who could replace him.

We might have to quit farming and call my daddy home to see what he thought about the situation.

(6)

Nate was late. He was always in the fields by six every morning but today we hadn't seen hide nor hair of him.

About 7:30 that morning me and Mama were in the barn feeding the stock when Nate's boy Billy came galloping up on Homer. He jerked him to a stop, dropped down and led him into the barn. He took his old sweat-stained hat off and walked up to Mama.

He stood there waiting for Mama to ask what he wanted.

"Where's your daddy, boy?" Mama asked.

"Beg pardon, Mrs. O'Rourke," he said, looking at the ground. "Daddy gone down with the miseries. Don't rightly know what. He said for me to tell you and see if maybe I could work in his place, that being alright with you ma'am."

Billy looked like a smaller and younger version of his daddy, except for two good eyes and his wide bare feet. His feet looked like two brown loafs of bread with toes. He had the same habit of shifting from one foot to the other as he talked and a slight bird sound that cheeped out of his mouth every once in a while when he paused to take a breath, just like his daddy.

"What have you been doing this summer, Billy?" Mama asked.

"I work on Mr. Thomas' farm until the miseries got him down, too, then he sold it to Mr. Barnes. He done fired us all and brought in his own hands to pick the crop." He took a red bandana out of his pocket and wiped his sweaty face.

"How old are you, Billy?" Mama said.

"Seventeen, ma'am. Going to join the paratroopers when I turn eighteen."

"I don't think they let colored join the paratroopers," Mama said.

"My Uncle Earl is in the paratroopers," I said. "He sent me a patch with a screaming eagle on it. Want to see it?"

Billy looked a bit dejected and began shifting his feet. "I seen one at the Army store. The man didn't say I couldn't be a paratrooper."

"I don't know for sure, that's just what I heard," Mama said.

"I think they have a place just for us colored," Billy said, looking sure of himself. He smiled, showing a missing tooth.

"What happened to your tooth, Billy?" I asked.

"Oh, that stupid mule threw his head back and caught me right in the mouth the other day."

Mama and I gave Homer a bad look. "Get a martingale on him when you ride and he can't do that," Mama said.

"Too late now, ma'am," Billy said and smiled, showing his missing tooth again.

"Alright Billy," Mama said. "Me and your daddy got a special crop deal, but I'll give you two dollars a day 'til your daddy gets back on his feet. Don't think I can afford two pickers, so when your daddy comes back I'll have to let you go."

"Sounds fair to me, ma'am," Billy said and wiped his face with his soiled red bandana again.

"All right," Mama said. "Let's get started."

Billy hooked Homer to the wagon and we worked close to sundown. Mama was real pleased with Billy's work.

"You did a good job, Billy. I'll see you tomorrow," she said.

"Yes'um," Billy said and headed Homer for the barn, pulling the wagon.

Billy unhitched Homer from the wagon, jumped up on him and took off. When he got to the main road, Henry appeared and motioned for him to stop. Billy pulled up Homer and she walked up and grabbed the reins. They talked for a few minutes but they were too far away for me to hear what they said. Billy spun his head back and forth like it was on a swivel, looking toward our house then the Barnes' place. Henry rubbed her hand on Billy's leg and laughed. He jerked the reins from her and lit out on Homer.

(7)

The next morning Billy was out in the field picking. It was just barely daylight when Mama and I got up.

Mama looked out the window and Billy was going after it. "I could use two like him," she said.

By the time we got a bite of breakfast and made it out to the fields Billy had ten bushel baskets of corn already on the wagon, and was picking more.

Mama looked at the corn on the wagon and shook her head. "You can slow down a might, Billy, you getting paid by the day."

"Yes'um, I know, but I promised I would help you pick this field and I was trying to get a day's work in early. My Daddy can't get around much now. Mama's trying to get on at the canning factory, but we don't know yet. I have to mend Mr. Barnes' fence. We need the money and he said I can't do it any day but today. I wanted you to get your money's worth before I had to leave."

"I think I already have. If you need to go, go on," Mama said. "I'm not in that big of a hurry. Tell you what, we'll call it a day and I'll pay you for the full day."

"No ma'am, I don't think I should do that. You're not getting your money's worth."

"Okay, you can make up the difference another time. When your daddy gets better."

"Yes ma'am. That would help, if you don't mind."

"That's fine. Take care of your family. If me and Trenton get it done before you can come back you can do something else."

"Yes ma'am. Let me know and I'll be here," he said. "You sure it ain't no bother, Mrs. O'Rourke?"

"I'm sure," she said and handed him a five dollar bill.

Billy looked at the five. "That's too much money, ma'am."

"No it's not," she said. "I just remembered I owe Nate three dollars."

He nodded and took the five. "Yes um," he said. "Forgive me, ma'am, I don't mean no disrespect, but I don't think you owe Daddy any money."

"A lot more than five dollars for all he's done for me," she said.

Billy smiled, showing his missing tooth, and stuck the five in his pocket.

"You can take Homer home, Billy. We'll throw a tarp over the corn and get in touch with you when we need to take it to the barn or wagon yard."

"Yes'um." He unhitched Homer from the wagon, climbed on him, waved and rode off. Henry didn't show up this time.

"I feel sorry for that boy," Mama said. "He's got a hard row to hoe. Being the oldest with his daddy down, he's got to make the livin' for his family. Being colored don't help him none, either."

(8)

I had just finished supper when I saw Beau through the front room window flying down the road, his curly blonde hair bouncing like coil springs as he ran. He was throwing up dust every time his bare feet hit the ground. His daddy usually didn't let him play after supper. He must have a good reason to take a chance on getting a whipping. Mama saw him coming, too. She was heating water for me to take a bath. She said to tell Beau to go home and come back tomorrow.

Beau came barreling into the yard, out of breath, with a scared look on his face. His blue eyes were as big as saucers.

He was yelling before he got to the door, "Tee, Tee, you in there!"

I met him on the front porch. "What're you doing here this late, Beau?"

"Daddy found the preacher dead in Mr. Barnes' barn a while ago," he said." I slipped off to tell you."

Mama heard what Beau said and walked out on the porch.

"What was that, laddie? The preacher has passed?" she said.

"Yes ma'am," Beau said, still trying to get his breath.

"What happened?" Mama said.

"Don't know," he said. "Daddy told me to go back in the house. I saw him though. His tongue was sticking out and I heard Daddy tell one of the hands he was dead."

"You be going on home now, laddie, before you get in trouble. Tell your papa me and Trenton can sit with Mrs. Barnes if she needs us. Sometimes it's hard to know what the good Lord's thinking, taking a preacher like that."

"Yes ma'am. See you later, Tee," Beau said.

"See you," I said. Beau jumped off the porch, put his feet in high gear, and set sail back home.

I'd never seen anyone dead before. I was supposed to go to the funeral of one of our relatives one time, but Daddy's car broke down so we didn't go.

I was still mulling over the idea of seeing a dead person when Mama yelled out for me to get on the back porch to take a bath. No sooner had I got there than she came out with a kettle of boiling water and a bar of Lysol soap.

"Trenton, get the tub and draw three buckets of water," she said. She wrapped the towel tighter around the kettle handle and set it on the floor. "Don't burn yourself. Take a bath and wash behind your ears. And put your clean over-alls on, we may be going to Mrs. Barnes' house."

"Yes ma'am," I said, and headed for the well.

A little while later after I took my bath, I was swinging on the front porch, getting cool, when Mr. Sterling came riding up on one of Mr. Barnes' paint horses. He tightened up on the reins, stopped in front of me, jumped off the horse and handed me the reins.

"Hold him for me, Tee," he said, stepping up on the porch. "Your grandma home?"

"Yes sir," I said, taking the reins.

Mama came to the front door and opened the screen. "Mr. Sterling?" she said. He removed his hat.

"Can I be of any help, sir?" Mama asked.

"Mrs. O'Rourke, I believe you can," he said.

It was for sure that Beau got his curly hair from his daddy, but Mr. Sterling didn't have much left on top. It was so smooth and shiny it looked like a good landing place for flies. Their blue eyes looked the same, except for Mr. Sterling's wrinkles. He was a big man with muscles to match. He was older than Daddy and his draft notice hadn't come up.

"Who's with the preacher?" Mama said.

"Mrs. Barnes and Mattie went to sit," he said. "Mrs. Barnes sent me to ask if you would help with the grievers. The preacher's entire congregation will probably be showing up at the house, and to the funeral, too. We are going to need some more help with the cooking."

"I'll be glad to. I can't believe he's gone," Mama said, rubbing her hands on her apron. "God rest his soul."

"Yes ma'am. Old Doc Crawford said he thinks it was a heart attack, but they won't know for sure until they have an au- au-topsy. I think that's what he said."

"Yes sir. I believe it's a doctor thing," Mama said. "When do you want me there?"

"Well," he said, scratching the top of his head. "Mrs. Barnes said the funeral was going to be Wednesday after the feeding. I'll pick you up that morning, around ten. That okay?"

"That's fine. What was the preacher doing in Mr. Barnes' barn?" Mama asked.

"Can't rightly say, ma'am. Mrs. Barnes told me to load some vegetables for her daddy, which I did. He said thank you, left the car, and headed for the barn without another word. Only time I ever saw him without a cigarette, except of course when he was preaching. I think I know why he was in the barn, but I can't talk about it in front of a lady."

"Oh, I see. Sorry," she said, blushing. "It's not for me to be asking," her hands going to the apron again.

"Well, got to go. Good day, ma'am," he said, putting his hat back on. "You know if Buzz is going to be here?" he asked.

"I don't think so. They still got cotton to pick and they will have to get it out of the field as soon as they can. We got some bad weather coming. I feel it in my bones."

"Yes ma'am. I'll see you Wednesday." Mama nodded.

I handed him the reins. He climbed up on the paint horse and took off.

That was the first time I ever thought about dying. What was I going to do? How long did I have?

(9)

Two days later, around ten in the morning, I saw Mr. Sterling in his Model A Ford bouncing down the sand road toward our house. That meant I got to ride in the rumble seat. The wind blowing in my face felt good on a hot summer day. Mama was dressed in her black funeral dress. She had her hair in a bun with a silver hair clasp holding it in place. She never wore make up. Mrs. Sterling tried to put lipstick and rouge on her one time. She wiped it off as soon as she looked in the mirror. She said she looked like a floozy. I had on my new overalls and last year's shoes that were already too tight and hurt my feet, but Mama said I had to wear them. She combed my hair but it wouldn't stay down so she put some lard on it.

Mr. Sterling pulled up to the porch, stopped and got out.

"Where's Mattie?" Mama asked.

"Mattie and the kids went on with Mrs. Barnes. I think they're going to have the feeding at noon, let the people visit with the preacher for a while, then have the funeral around three this afternoon." It looked like I was going to see my first dead person and it was going to be the preacher. My stomach wasn't too happy about it. I thought I was going to throw up all over Mr. Sterling's rumble seat before we got there.

The church was right next to the preacher's house and the parking lot was full of cars and wagons just like Mr. Sterling said it would be. The white clapboard church was one big room with ten rows of pews and a stained mahogany pulpit. A baptism room was behind the pulpit with a big window so you could see who was being baptized. I was baptized there when I was six years old. A dining hall was attached to the back of the church and both had indoor water fixtures, a toilet and electricity. The preacher didn't have to pay for any of it. Daddy said maybe he should become a preacher because everybody was always giving you things.

Mrs. Taylor was playing "Amazing Grace" on the piano when we pulled in.

Mr. Sterling drove up to the open double doors of the church, stopped, cut the engine off, got out and opened the door for Mama. I jumped out of the rumble seat behind her.

"You wait outside, laddie, until I find out where you're supposed to go," Mama said.

"You mean I'm not going in?"

"Not yet."

I tried to act disappointed, but I was glad. I wasn't sure I was ready to see a dead person.

Sheriff Charlie Bowman was standing by the door saying howdy to everyone who came in the church. Election was coming up and it was not unusual to see him at a funeral of someone he didn't even know, politicking.

My aunt Sara Beth showed up a little later in her almost-new DeSoto. She was dressed in black like all the other women, but she had on a shiny diamond necklace, rings and a bracelet. Her dress was kind of tight. Daddy said it was her looks that hooked Tim Newberry, one of the richest men in town. "Pretty women can do those kinds of things to a man," he had said. "Make him forget his own name if he's not careful." She made sure people knew she had money, wearing all that jewelry. She never gave us a dime. Tim Newberry got run over by a train the first year they were married. She got the Newberry Candy factory and the fortune. His family tried to get it back, but they couldn't. Daddy said the only thing she had going for her as far as he was concerned was she helped raise my mother, who was five years younger than my aunt.

She sashayed up to the open church doors and saw me standing there, paused and looked at me.

"Tee," she said, matter-of-fact, and stroked the top of my head a couple of times like she did that Persian cat of hers, and walked on in the church. I watched her from the door as she walked down the aisle, her high heels clicking on the floor. I never figured out how females could walk in those things. She walked past the coffin, glanced at the preacher and sat down in a pew beside Doc Crawford's wife.

I saw Beau peeking in the church window and crept up behind him.

"What're you doing, Beau Sterling?" I said, punching him in the ribs.

He jumped and pushed me.

"Don't do that," he said. "I was trying to get a look in the coffin."

"Why don't you just go in and look at him," I said.

"Daddy said for me to stay out here until he got ready for me to come in."

"That's what Mama told me."

"Look through right here and you can see him," he said, putting his finger against the window pane.

I looked through the window. All I could see was Mrs. Taylor's chubby fingers playing the piano. The preacher's wife was sitting in a chair by the casket with two big fans blowing on her. She looked awful small and her gray hair had turned snow white. Her hands were trembling. She was already old, but she looked even older now. It wouldn't be long until I would be going to her funeral. Mrs. Barnes was sitting next to her mother, her husband next to her. Their son Ethan was sitting in the back pew about half asleep, or drunk, we weren't sure which. They had another son but he was off fighting in the war. Mrs. Barnes was probably as old as Mama. She always had an asthma thing with her. She was really puffing on it today. She was a nice lady. I liked her. She would bring me cookies and milk when we went to the hoedowns in Mr. Barnes' barn.

The casket lid was open, but I couldn't see him. He was too far down in the casket.

"You can't see him from here, Beau. He's sunk into the casket."

"You ain't looking right, Tee, I can see him." Beau was looking in the window, his hands covering his eyes like horse blinders to shield them from the sunlight.

"Well, I can see him," he said.

"You cannot. You're just saying that because you want to tell everybody you saw a dead person."

"No I'm not," he said. "You need to have your eyes fixed. You can't see nothin'."

I stuck my nose back against the dirty window pane and saw Mrs. Barnes bent over, kissing the preacher in the coffin. A chill ran through me. I moved back from the window and leaned up against the wall, my knees trying to buckle.

"How could anyone do that," I said, sweat popping out on my forehead.

"Do what?" Beau said. He was looking at me with a strange look. "You're white as a sheet, Tee. What's the matter?"

"Mrs. Barnes was kissing the preacher."

"That's her daddy," Beau said.

"But he's dead," I said.

"You're a sissy, Tee."

"I am not."

"I dare you to go in and touch him," Beau said.

"Mama told me to stay out here until she came for me."

"You are scared," he said.

"I gotta find Mama," I said

"You're a fraidy cat, you're a fraidy cat," Beau said.

"I ain't talking to you," I said, and left him looking through the window.

When I walked around the corner of the church I saw Willie Alcott standing real close to Henry, smiling at her. He was rubbing his leg against hers. Willie was way too old for Henry. He dropped out of school three years ago and had been working at Mr. Tucker's store ever since. His dad was always drunk and his mother ran off with a traveling shoe salesman. He had been living in an upstairs apartment above the store, working for Mr. Tucker, waiting to be drafted ever since.

His hands were as big as a pitcher's mitt, and he was maybe 200 pounds, six-feet-tall, with legs as big around as my waist. He wore thick glasses and a short crew cut. He claimed he tried to join the Marines but got turned down because of his eyes. Anytime Mr. Tucker had trouble with someone he would call Willie and it didn't take long for the trouble to go away.

Henry was dressed in a black dress with the top cut out. I guess you could call her pretty. She had long blonde hair, big blue eyes. Her face painted up, black mesh stockings and shiny black high heel shoes with buckles on them. As close as Willie was standing to her I knew he could see much more than he should.

Two women I didn't know were looking at Henry and Willie. One was tall, gray-headed and skinny, with a black scarf tied around her neck; the other one short and fat, with a double chin and bulging eyes. They reminded me of a female Mutt and Jeff.

I heard the fat one say, "That's a disgrace. That girl come to a man of the cloth's funeral dressed like a floozy, letting that boy rub all over her. Doesn't she have any decency?"

"Guess not," the skinny one said. "Her papa needs to take a switch to her."

I think Henry heard them. She didn't say anything, but she gave them the evil eye and moved away from Willie. The two women stared right back and Henry dropped her head and went inside the church. I wondered if Mr. Sterling knew how she was dressed.

I could see people passing by the preacher's casket, but I didn't see Mama.

Mrs. Gates stuck her head out the preacher's kitchen door and said "Tee, come here."

Mrs. Gates was my homeroom teacher. Daddy said she looked like a female wrestler to him and could probably whip half the men in town. She was married to a truck driver once, but he up and disappeared. No one ever knew what happened to him. Mrs. Gates said he just took off and everyone accepted that, including the sheriff.

"Tee, you and Beau pass the word: dinner's ready in the banquet hall for anyone who wants to eat," she said.

"Yes ma'am," I said and started looking for Beau.

Beau still had his face pressed against the window. "Hey Beau," I said.

"What you want, Tee?"

"Why don't you just go inside and see him if you're that bent on doing it," I said.

"'Cause I was told to stay outside, too. Only I'm not a scaredy cat like you are."

"Beau, sometimes you sure can be aggravating. Mrs. Gates says for us to pass the word that dinner's ready."

Beau took off running toward the banquet hall.

"Where are you going, you're supposed to help me."

"I'm hungry, you do it," he said and kept running.

I made the rounds in and out of the church by myself, making sure I didn't go near the preacher, telling people dinner was ready and they started going into the banquet hall where Mama and the other ladies had set up the food.

I had just told some newcomers in the parking lot about dinner when I saw Mr. Sterling come out of the church holding Henry by the arm. He was squeezing her arm and she was trying to pull away. He marched her to the Model A and pushed her in and closed the door. She tried to open the door and he slapped her. She didn't move after that, and they took off. Mrs. Mutt and Jeff came to the door of the church and stood there, smiling at each other. They watched the Model A until it disappeared over a hill.

After dinner, Beau and I were out in the parking lot knocking marbles out of a ring with our tops when Mama came out and said it was time.

We went in the church and sat down far enough back that I still couldn't see in the coffin. Some preacher I hadn't seen before preached Brother Callaway's funeral and we all got up and walked past the casket. I closed my eyes when I got to the casket and walked on past. No one but me knew I never looked at him.

Mrs. Barnes got Ethan to drive us home. He had long shaggy brown hair and sideburns down the side of his face. I heard Mr. Barnes tell him one time to cut his hair, but he didn't. He said he was like Samson; his strength was in his hair. He told everyone that. He thought it was funny. No one knew what Ethan might do next.

Sometimes when Mama and I went to church he would be sitting in a back pew asleep, snoring bigger than Ike. Being the preacher's grandson, no one would wake him up and the preacher ignored him and kept on preaching. I could tell Mama wasn't too happy about Ethan driving us home, but that was the only ride we had. It was the first time I ever rode in a convertible. Ethan worked as a foreman on his daddy's farm but sometime he would disappear for days and no one knew where he was.

The rumor was his daddy paid off a draft board member and had him declared mentally unstable to be in the Army. Ethan was 28 years old, had a college education and had never done anything. He stayed drunk most of the time and lived off his family.

Mama said his problem was he didn't know the Lord. The Barnes' other son, Cody, was Mr. Barnes' pride and joy. Cody was a captain in the Army Air Force and flew fighters. Mr. Barnes was always bragging on him, but I never heard him say anything good about Ethan.

On the way home, Mr. Sterling passed us going back toward the church with Henry, wearing a different dress and her face wiped clean. I could tell Mama felt better when we turned down the road to the house. I did too. It sure would feel good to get those tight shoes off.

We came to a stop and Ethan got out and opened the door for Mama, and I got out behind her.

"Thank you, Ethan, for the ride home," Mama said.

"You're welcome, Mrs. O'Rourke," he said, got back in his convertible and drove away.

"Guess we won't be going to church for a while," I said.

"Why do you say that?" Mama said.

"We don't have a preacher," I said.

"Oh, we'll have a preacher. One will visit the church until we find a new one."

I was going to have to wear those tight shoes again.

(10)

I waited on Beau for over an hour the next morning. We always went fishing before eight in the morning while it was cool. I was ready to give up when I saw him running across the pasture. He put on the brakes as he hit the front yard. His eyes were red, like he had been bawling.

"You get a smacking for something, Beau?" I said.

"No. We going fishing?" he said, raising his hand to his face, making a double swipe across his eyes, then his nose, in one motion.

"You're awful late," I said.

"Alright, if you don't want to go I'll go home."

"I didn't say I didn't want to go. I just said you were late."

"If we're going, let's dig some worms and go," he said. "I got to be home by noon to help Mama peel taters."

"Looks like you have been bawling about something to me."

Beau batted his eyes, another tear appeared, and he quickly wiped it away.

"What's wrong?" I said. "I'm your best friend. You can tell me. I won't tell. I cross my heart," I said, making an X across my chest.

"Daddy's going to send Henry to the reform school," he said. "He said he don't know what else to do with her. I don't want her to go."

"What's wrong with her going to a special school?"

"You don't even know what a reform school is, do you, Tee?"

"Well, no. I guess it's like the name, some kind of school."

"It ain't no school. It's like a jail and you can't get out. I might never see her again."

"If it ain't a school then why do they call it one?"

"Because it's a place they lock you up, treat you bad, and make you go to school too."

"You can't get out?" I said

"No," Beau said and wiped his face with the back of his hand and turned his head away.

"You want me to ask Mama if she would talk to your daddy?"

"About what?"

"About Henry. Maybe she can change his mind. She's a good persuader."

"Daddy might not like that," he said.

"What you going to do?"

"I don't know," he said. "My Mama is going to talk to him. Maybe she can change his mind."

"Yeah that's what my daddy always says, 'If anybody can change a man's mind it's a woman.'"

"I don't want to talk about it anymore," he said. "Are we going fishing or not?"

"Yep, but it's too late to dig worms. They gone down deep by now with it getting so hot. We'll have to catch some grasshoppers, instead," I said. "You catch the grasshoppers and I'll have Mama make us a sandwich to take with us."

"Why do I always have to catch the grasshoppers?"

"You want to talk to Mama about the sandwich?"

"No."

"Then catch the grasshoppers. There's a jar in the barn."

"Oh alright, hurry up." Beau kicked at the dirt and headed for the barn.

Mama was boiling cabbage when I went in the house. I stood there until she asked me what I wanted.

"Mama what's a reform school?" I asked.

"It's a place where they put bad kids."

"Can they get out?"

"Not until their folks say they can, unless of course they have done something against the law, then it's up to a judge."

"How do you know about them?" I asked, surprised.

"Glenda Gates' family had to put her in one for a whole year. She was wild as a deer when she was a girl."

"Well, looks like she's okay. Didn't hurt her none."

"No, if anything it helped her. She found out she had to follow rules like everyone else. What's this about, laddie? Is there something on your mind?"

"Oh, nothing. I just wanted to know. Would you make me and Beau a sandwich? We're going fishing for a while."

"Alright, but be careful. Creek's up. Better take your .22 in case a moccasin shows up. Peanut butter and jelly be all right?" she said.

"Yes ma'am, that's fine," I said. That wasn't one of my favorites, but I would take what I could get.

Mama got the peanut butter and jelly, whipped up two sandwiches in a few seconds, put them in a paper sack, and handed me the sandwiches and a jar for water.

"Run along. Bring me enough perch for your supper."

I liked fried fish. "I'll catch some big ones. Can we have corn meal muffins and buttermilk with them?"

"Sure laddie. The cabbage will be done by then, too. Beau can have supper with us."

"Yes ma'am." I said, and hurried off to get the fishing poles.

Beau wasn't having much luck catching the grasshoppers so I had to help him. He didn't have his mind on it. We chased grasshoppers for thirty minutes until we figured we had enough. I was about ready to forget it and try another day, but I thought fishing might help Beau feel better. I still wasn't sure what all a reform school was but it sure sounded like someplace you didn't want to be. I could understand why Beau was so worried. I know I would be if I had a sister. Mr. Sterling should find another way to get Henry to do what he wanted. Although I didn't have any idea what that would be. Maybe I was better off being by myself. I didn't have to worry about stuff like that. Although I would like a puppy to play with.

(11)

The creek was a five minute walk from the house, down a white sand road with bushes alongside. Old spread-natters would show up and chase you. Beau said if they caught you they would grab on to your leg and chew it off. Mama said that was just an old wives' tale, they didn't do that and they weren't poisonous, they were bluffing to get you to leave. I hated those snakes. They would spread out their head like one of them cobras I saw in movies, and come a-running at you. I never hung around to find out which story was true. I would take off like a blue streak and they would give up chasing me after a little ways and disappear into the grass.

Another thing we had to watch out for was bull nettles. Those things would sting you 'til the skin turned bright red, and itched so much you could hardly stand it. I got into one once and almost scratched my leg off it itched so much. There was something good about them, though. They had little almond-like nuts that grew in the middle of the yellow flowers on them. If I got hungry I would carefully pick some flowers off them and eat the nuts. You had to be real hungry to take the chance.

We saw two toad frogs hooping along the side of the path. That was a bad sign. The snakes ate them, and lay in wait as they hopped along, but we didn't see any spread-natters today. They were probably curled up under a bush by now. Even a snake got hot in the Mississippi heat.

We put a grasshopper on our hook, sat down on a log over the creek and waited. An old owl showed up and began hooting his head off. Owls were supposed to come out at night. This one must've had his days and nights mixed up. I threw a stick at him. He just looked at me and kept on hooting. The fish weren't biting and it was probably because of that darn old owl. He wouldn't shut his big mouth.

The snake doctors began swarming around, too close for comfort. That meant a water moccasin was nearby. That made me nervous. I sure didn't want one of them two-steppers to bite me. Mama said the ones around Sugar Creek were poisonous and that was why they called them two-steppers. If one bit you, two steps and you were dead.

I didn't know if it was the owl's fault or not, but I wasn't catching any fish. Beau didn't have his mind on fishing. He was still thinking about his sister Henry. It wasn't long until he laid the pole down and was off exploring the arrowhead beds downstream. Uncle Earl told me the Choctaws used to camp there and shrink the raw hides on the arrow shanks in the creek. Sometimes they would leave some. Most people didn't know that the Indians had different kinds of arrows for hunting different kinds of game. Uncle Earl showed me the ones for bigger game. They were larger, longer and narrow. The smaller ones for birds and rabbits were shorter and thinner.

I finally gave up fishing, too, and was taking the line off the pole when the sun broke through the clouds and shined down on a little nook a ways down the creek. Something was splashing in a small pool off from the main water. I walked the log I had been sitting on back to the bank and walked down the bank of the creek for a closer look. That's when I saw him.

It was the biggest catfish I had ever seen. He must have been as long as I was tall and his head was bigger than mine. He had mud rolled up around the hole where he had been splashing. I could see the top of his head and tail sticking out of the water. He had got himself in a heck of a mess. He must have been hanging out in the shallow water, eating small fish, and couldn't get out when the water went down.

I picked up my .22 and aimed. Somehow it didn't seem right to shoot him. I laid the gun down, tied the line back on a pole, and flung the fishing line in front of him with a big fat juicy grasshopper dangling on it He ignored the grasshopper and kept splashing around in the small pool. I guess he was too depressed to eat. The water was barely deep enough for him to breathe. Soon the oxygen would be gone and he would die. He kept splashing around but it wasn't going to do him any good. The creek was too far away, he would just wind up on dry land. He was so big, he must be a smart fish to have lived this long, at least until now.

All I had to do was pull the trigger, but I couldn't do it. Catching him on a hook was the way it was supposed to happen. I laid the rifle down and made my way down to the little nook. I stepped off into the soft mud burying up to my knees, and grabbed him by the tail. I couldn't budge him.

"Beau," I yelled. "Come here!" He didn't answer. "Beau, you hear me?" I called again.

"Yeah, I hear you," he yelled back. "What you want?"

"I want you to come here. I found something."

"What is it?"

"Just come here."

I heard Beau splashing across the shallow water of the creek toward me.

He saw the catfish and stopped in his tracks.

"Holy cow," he said, his eyes glued to the fish. "That must be the biggest catfish ever."

"Well, probably not ever, but he is a big one," I said. "Help me get him back in the creek."

"Back in the creek! Are you crazy, Tee? We're going to take him home."

"No we're not. It ain't fair to catch him like this."

"Who cares," Beau said. "You got the biggest fish ever come out of Sugar Creek, wait 'til your grandma sees him."

"She ain't going to. You're going to help me drag him to the creek. And besides, how would we get him home, anyway. He's too big to carry."

"I'll go get my wagon," Beau said, stepping off into the mud next to me. He squatted down and stroked the fish on the head like he was a puppy.

"What you doing, Beau?"

"I just wanted to touch him. He sure would be good eating."

"No. Now help me drag him to the creek. We're going to let him go. I found him so he's my fish, right?"

"He's your fish, but I sure wouldn't let him go."

"Well I would, now help me."

It took every bit of strength Beau and I had to drag him to the creek bank. He turned his head and looked at the water, raised himself up with his tail and rolled off into the creek and was gone. I wasn't sure I had done the right thing. I know I would have felt guilty eating him. I took a look at the place the fish had disappeared into the water.

"We're not telling Mama about the catfish, Beau, you got me?"

"Yeah, I got you. She would think you were crazy, anyway, just like I do."

"Keep your mouth shut," I said, grabbing him by his shirt. "I wouldn't want to have to beat you up."

"You couldn't anyway, but I'll keep quiet."

"You promise?"

"Yeah, I told you I would."

"We might as well go on home then," I said.

"I need to run. It helps me think," Beau said.

"Whatever, just keep your mouth shut about the fish."

"Don't worry," he said, breaking into a run. He turned and ran backwards, yelling at me. "Your grandma would probably blame me for letting you be such a softy."

"Go home, Beau. We'll meet at the tree in the morning and go hunting instead of fishing."

"Okay with me," he said.

In a few seconds Beau had disappeared down the sand road.

Mama was looking for fish when I got home.

"I'm sorry, Mama. I didn't catch any. They wouldn't bite today."

"That's alright," she said. "I got some good beans cooked, and your cornbread. I can fry some salt meat with it if you like. The cabbage is done, and I got you and Beau a big glass of buttermilk."

"He had to get on home," I said. "Can I eat later, please ma'am. I'm not hungry right now."

"Did Beau tell you about Henry?" Mama said.

"How did you know?"

"That talk about reform school. Mattie told me all about it sometime back. She was worried sick. Seems like Henry has gone plum wild. She's been slipping off, going down to colored town to listen to that blues music, drink home brew at those jive joints, and heaven knows what else. White girls don't go down there unless they're looking for trouble. Mattie tried to keep it from Mr. Sterling, but one of the hired hands told him. He sure was upset with Mattie. He's been threatening to kick both of them out. Henry had a bruise on her face. She said she walked into a door, but maybe not. Best you stay out of it. It's a family matter, and you ain't family. I feel bad for her, but she made her own bed, now she has to sleep in it. That's what happens when you forget

63

the Almighty and think you can sin and get away with it. Remember that, Trenton. Always put the good Lord first."

I nodded.

Mama wiped her hands on her apron and sat my plate and the food on the table.

I wasn't sure what sin Henry committed, but if Mama said she did, I guess she did. I sat down, poured a glass of buttermilk and dug in. That catfish was probably a mile down the creek by now.

(12)

I met Beau at the big tree the next morning. That old oak tree was as big around as a car and was probably there when Sherman marched through Angel Point. Everyone knew about the old tree and just referred to it as "The Tree." It was on the edge of our land and the old Foster place. Old Man Foster died three years ago and his sister in California inherited it, but never came to claim it. Daddy said it was just a matter of time until Mr. Barnes bought it.

Beau sat down and took a big piece of chocolate cake out of a sack and handed me half. We ate cake and talked about Henry for a while. He said his daddy had backed off a little, telling her if she stayed away from them jive joints he would teach her how to drive a car.

"That was my mama's idea," Beau said. "If she doesn't, then he will take her to Vicksburg and leave her there until she's 18 and she can do whatever she wants, except come home."

"Sounds pretty mean to me," I said.

"Yeah, well Daddy said he's tired of messin' with her."

After we finished off the cake it was time to go hunting.

"The best place to go is down by the creek on the Foster place," Beau said. "No one has been hunting there since Old Man Foster died. They should be bouncing around like popcorn."

"No, we better stay here," I said. "Daddy said I wasn't supposed to hunt anywhere except on our land, and some clouds are rollin' in. We may get rained on before we could even get to the Foster place."

"We ain't going to be there very long," Beau said. "We'll be gone before the rain comes. Your daddy's not going to know?"

"I'll know."

"You're an old scaredy cat, Tee. You're afraid to do anything. You act like a baby."

"I do not. I just don't think it's a good idea. If Daddy finds out he'll take my rifle away, and I bet your daddy would do the same to you."

"My Daddy doesn't care where I hunt. He knows I can take care of myself. That's the difference between me and you, Tee. Are you coming or not?"

"No."

"Suit yourself." Beau stood up, slung his rifle strap across his shoulder and started walking away.

I stood there watching him get further away. "All right!" I yelled. "I'm coming, but you better not tell anyone."

"Of course not." He grinned and brushed his hair out of his face.

"We'll kill two. Mama said she would cook them and you could eat with us if you wanted to."

"I'll kill as many as I want to," Beau said, defiantly.

"Then I'm gone right now. We eat what we kill and no more."

"You think the squirrels are going to know? They're all going to be gone by the time we're grown anyway."

"Maybe so, but it won't be me that helps it a long."

"You been listening to your daddy again. He sure acts mighty big to be a cotton picker."

"Take that back," I said, shoving Beau.

"I ain't taking anything back."

"I'm going to smack you, Beau Sterling. Put your dukes up."

I laid my rifle down and waited for Beau to do the same. Instead, he just stood there, his rifle resting on his shoulder, looking at me like I had suddenly lost my mind. After a few long seconds of staring at each other, Beau shook his head.

"Okay, I'm sorry, no sense in fighting. Although, I would whip you good, Tee."

"No way," I said.

Beau shook his head again and turned away.

"One of these days we're going to find out who can whip who," I said. "Might as well be now."

Beau didn't say anything and walked away. I waited for my temper to cool down and caught up to him.

"Alright, two squirrels. And I didn't mean that about your daddy," Beau said. He spit on his hand and stuck it out for me to shake. I looked at his gooey hand then shook it.

"Okay, forget it." I looked up and saw the old Foster well directly in front of us.

"You see that, Beau? It looks like someone has been down here not too long ago. There's tire tracks down the road to the well. I didn't think anyone ever came down here anymore."

"Ain't anyone lived in the house since Mr. Foster died," Beau said. He wrinkled up his nose. "You smell anything, Tee?"

"Yeah, it's strong. Don't see anything, no buzzards, must be in the well."

"Help me slide the top off, Tee, and let's see what it is."

"I don't know, we might better leave it alone."

"See, there you go again. You're afraid to do anything," Beau said.

"I am not. Get beside me and we'll push together," I said.

Beau moved around the curb and we both put our hands on the cover, gave a heave-ho and the cover slid off. The smell swept over us like a skunk convention. I threw up on the side of the well. Beau turned away and did the same on the ground.

"Boy, whatever that is, it's putting out a terrible stench," Beau said.

"Let's see what it is," I said.

"Are you kidding? I'm not sticking my head in that well," Beau said, pulling his shirt up over his mouth.

"Now who's the 'fraidy cat? You're the one wanted to look in the well," I said.

"Okay, you go first. Let's see you do it," Beau said, pushing me toward the well.

I jerked my shirt up over my nose and looked in. Sunlight ran down one side of the well, almost to the water. Something was floating in the well. It rolled over slightly and I saw two big eyes, almost out of their sockets, staring at me. It was a naked body with a rope tied around its neck. My eyes adjusted to the light and I could see it was a colored girl. Some of the skin was missing from her face.

"Holy shit," I said and staggered back from the well.

"What!" Beau said. "What is it?"

"It's a body. Looks like a colored girl fell in the well. We got to go get the sheriff."

"No wait," Beau said. "We don't have to tell. Let someone else find her."

"Beau, you need some real serious teaching about right and wrong. Of course we got to tell. It's a body. You stay here and I'll go fetch Mr. Barnes so he can call the sheriff."

"Why do I have to stay here? She ain't going anywhere."

I looked at Beau with a puzzled look. "I don't know. Come on, then, let's get out of here."

We both took off running. Beau had already told Mr. Barnes what happened before I got there.

"You boys better wait for the sheriff," he said. "He may want to ask you some questions."

It was almost an hour before Sheriff Bowman showed up. We got in his car and he drove us to the well. We showed him the dead girl.

"Did you go in the house?" he asked.

"No sir," I said. "I don't think you can get in. They got the windows and doors nailed shut."

"I'll have a look. Don't be bringing your friends down here to show off," the sheriff said. "I'm going to have the coroner's office in Vicksburg pick her up and run some tests. You boys stay away from here. You hear me?"

"You don't have to worry about us, Mr. Bowman," I said. "Me and Beau ain't never coming here again. Right, Beau?" Beau nodded in agreement.

A clap of thunder made me jump.

"Looks like we got some weather coming," the sheriff said. "Maybe the coroner can get her out before the rain comes. You two better run on home and tell your folks what happened. Thanks for calling me."

"Yes sir," I said, and we lit out for home.

When I got home I told Mama what we found and what the sheriff had said.

"Don't you go down there no more," she said. "You shouldn't have gone there in the first place. I don't know if I should tell your daddy or not."

"He'll take my rifle away," I said.

"May paddle your hind end. I'll think about it," she said and wiped her hands on her apron.

(13)

It was a little before dawn when the tapping on the tin roof woke me, which wasn't all bad. I was having a bad dream about those eyes staring at me in the well. The rain was coming down hard. Lightning was streaking across the sky every few seconds and the wind was sweeping the dirt in the backyard like a broom. The thunder came in waves and made the whole house shake. Then, just as quick as it came, it was gone. The thunder stopped. The wind died, and it stopped raining. It was as quiet as a Monday morning church. Then it all started up again. The rain came back in blinding sheets of water. The thunder roared, the house shook, and the lightning flashed across the sky, lighting up the early morning for miles.

Mama came out on the porch. "Get up, Trenton, a twister's coming! We got to get to the cellar."

I jumped up, slipped on my overalls and we headed for the cellar. Mama had her fruit jar of money and a lit lantern.

"Hurry," she said, "we don't have much time."

"What about the animals and chickens?"

"No time, go."

By the time we reached the cellar door, the wind was so strong it was all we could do to stand, and we couldn't get the cellar door open. Mama set the lantern down to pull on the door and the lantern blew away. She held on to her money jar with one hand and pulled on the door with the other. I was pulling with both hands. A gust of wind ran under it and it flew open so fast it almost gave Mama another scar on her chin. We grabbed the rope tied to the cellar door, jumped off the steps and hung on, dropping down in the cellar and pulling the door shut with our weight into knee-deep water.

"See if you can find the bar in the corner, laddie, to latch the door. Hurry, I'll hang on."

I waded through the water and felt around for the bar. I yelled as loud as I could, trying to be heard over the roar of the twister. "It's not here!"

"Try the other corner," she yelled, "Hurry!"

The door was bouncing up and down, Mama hanging on for dear life, the door bopping her on the head several times.

I found the bar and ran it through the braces.

"Thank the Lord," she said. "I was about out of strength."

A sound like an oncoming freight train got louder and louder until we had to hold our hands over our ears the sound was so deafening. We could hear the trees falling and splats of something hitting the cellar door. The water was pouring in around the door, rising fast. We were up to our waists in water. If it kept coming in we would drown. Morning shades of light began to creep through the cracks in the cellar door. A snake slithered across the water to the other side of the cellar and disappeared.

"He's as scared as we are," Mama said.

"I doubt that," I said.

The door quit bouncing and the roaring stopped. Everything got quiet again.

"Take the bar out," she said. "I think we can get out now."

We made our way out of the cellar as quick as possible and looked around. Several chickens had splattered against the cellar door, barn and the house. Chicken guts, blood, and feathers were stuck to walls everywhere. The pigs and cow were gone. The barn roof was gone. The well curb was missing. It looked like almost everything blew away, except the house.

The old house was still standing. Only one piece of the tin roof was missing. The twister had shot pine needles into trees like bullets no more than fifty yards from the house. It had made a right turn from the house, straight across the fields.

It took a minute for that to sink in. Then it hit me. There was nothing in the fields, no pea vines or corn, stalks, nothing. The entire crop had disappeared like magic in a matter of minutes, every acre wiped clean as a whistle. Nothing but dirt. Three months of hard work gone in minutes, and with it, the money it would have brought in.

(14)

The next day we were cleaning up the best we could when I saw Daddy's old Chevy turn off the main road, headed for the house. I ran out to the clothesline to tell Mama. She picked up the clothes basket and went in the house. I took off for the front yard to wait for him.

He pulled up by the front porch and cut the engine. I ran to the car and jumped up on the running board.

"Hi son, I missed you," he said.

"I missed you, too," I said.

Mama walked out in the yard next to the car. "What you doing home, Buzz? I thought there was a couple more weeks of picking?"

"Mr. Barnes called Old Man Tillie to tell me about the twister. Figured I better get home. The cotton's about gone anyway."

I stood on the running board, looking in with my mouth open. There was a big package on the back seat.

Daddy came around the car to where I was. He looked as big and strong as ever. He reminded me of the wedding picture of grandpa. They looked a lot alike.

"I brought you something." A big grin spread across his face, and his eyes sparkled.

I knew it was something special. "What is it?"

"Open it," he said.

I dove in the car and hurriedly unwrapped the package, then I saw it. It almost took my breath away. It was the motor airplane from the mercantile store.

Daddy saw my excitement and smiled. "Well, what do you think?"

"Thank you, Daddy! I'll keep it forever."

"As soon as we get time, we'll take it out to the pasture and give it a spin," he said. "Go ahead, get it out of the car and bring it up on the porch and we'll take a look."

Mama shook her head and walked back in the house.

I didn't realize at the time how difficult it was for him to buy that airplane. Twenty-five dollars was a lot of money in the cotton fields.

I was so excited about my new airplane it was hard to keep the smile off my face. I slept with it on a pillow next to me that night and would wake up during the night and check to see if it was still there.

The next morning Daddy and Mama woke me with their loud talking.

"We're fine, Buzz. Mr. Barnes should mind his own business." Mama's apron was getting a workout. "I knew you were going to try and get me to sell the place. I'm not."

"The twister wiped out your crop. You don't have anything to make any money. I went down there to pick cotton because I could make more than working on the farm, but that's over, and we don't have a crop. I got to find something to make a livin'."

"I got some money," she said.

"Mama, I don't want to upset you, but that little bit of money you got won't last six months. You're used to raising ninety percent of your livelihood but you don't have time to grow it back, even if you could. It's going to take two hundred dollars just to fix the barn. I want to sell the farm and move on. I heard about a good job with the government in Oakridge, Tennessee. A friend of mine can get me on. It's supposed to help the war effort and we could forget about all this. Put it behind us. Nobody can make a living on a small farm anymore. You're living in the past. Earl's not going to farm anymore. He told me when he got back he was going to ask Mary Ann Spencer to marry him and get out of Angel Point as fast as he could. He wants to better himself, not spend the rest of his life using a mule's butt for a compass, and I don't blame him."

"This is my life, and this is my farm until I die. Earl never said anything to me about leaving, but that's his choice and yours, too. You and Earl can do what you want. I'm going to replant the same forty acres and grow a new crop. I'll get starter plants to speed it up. You can go if you want to, but Trenton will be better off with me."

"You know I can't do that, Mama. Please think it over and we'll talk some more."

"There's no 'thinking it over' to do," she said and left the room.

Daddy walked out on the back porch and rolled a cigarette. I pretended to be asleep.

"I know you're not asleep, young man. I got a bone to pick with you, too."

"What did I do?" I said, throwing the cover off.

"Well, for one thing, you went hunting on someone else's land. Charlie Bowman told me about you and Beau finding that colored girl in the well when I got into town."

"The sheriff's got a big mouth. I agree with Mama, a lot of people around here talk too much."

"You watch yours, young man. Put your .22 in the closet and don't take it out until I say so, and don't be running off anywhere. They don't know what happened to her."

"It was Beau's fault," I said. "He didn't want to tell anyone about the dead nigger girl, but I told him we had to, even though I knew you would find out."

"It's always easy to blame someone else when you're in trouble. And don't call them that again. That's a word they hate."

"Everyone else does," I said.

"Not everyone. Nate said it was wrong, like they were still slaves. From now on you call them colored or I'll tan your britches."

"Yes sir. When can I get my .22 back?"

"I don't know. We'll see. In the meantime we can go fly that new airplane."

"Let's go. I'll get it," I said. All of a sudden the .22 wasn't as important as it was a minute ago.

"Take it out to the pasture," Daddy said. "I'll be right there as soon as I siphon a little gas out of the car to put in the motor. We can't use much. I don't have any more gas stamps for this month."

That darn airplane could fly like a real one. I hung on to the guide wire and made it climb, dive and just fly. It was the best present I ever got. I would always remember it and what I did with it.

(15)

I was checking out my airplane on the porch when I saw Nate's boy Billy come flying out of the woods, running like the devil was after him. He ran up to me all out of breath. His overalls had holes tore in the knees. Grass burrs were sticking in his pant legs.

"Mr. Tee, I need to talk to Mrs. O'Rourke." He was breathing hard and his eyes were big as saucers.

Mama heard him and came out into the yard. Daddy followed.

"What's wrong, Billy?" Mama asked.

"Mrs. O'Rourke, I'm in big trouble. It's about Miss Henry, seems somebody said I kissed her, but I didn't, she kissed me. Now Mr. Sterling and a bunch more white folks are coming after me."

"Did you, Billy? Tell me the truth."

"I didn't kiss her. She kissed me. She just walked up and kissed me slapdab on the mouth before I knew what was goin' on."

Billy backed away from Daddy, like he was expecting him to pounce on him.

"It's alright, boy," Daddy said. "You need to get to town and talk to Charlie Bowman. He's a fair man."

"Yes sir, he is, but I would never make it to town. Mr. Sterling and them other men goin' to hurt me bad if they catch me. I ain't done nothin', I swear. She kissed me. Mr. Moore saw her. I don't mean no disrespect, but he lied and told Mr. Sterling I was the one doing the kissing, and you know what happens to a colored boy in Mississippi when he gets too friendly with a white girl."

Billy looked at Mama. "Miss Henry wouldn't tell them any different now they going to hurt me, Mrs. O'Rourke. I got no place to go. They would listen to you, ma'am."

"I don't think so, Billy." Mama looked down at Billy's bare feet. "Wait here," she said, and hurried in the house.

"Where's your daddy, boy?" Daddy asked.

"He's down with the miseries. He told me to come here for help, that I need a white person to talk for me."

"I believe you, Billy," Daddy said, "but the best thing for you to do, if you won't go to the sheriff, is to get out of Angel Point."

Billy began shuffling his feet, looking at the house.

"What's your grandma doing, Mr. Tee? I can't wait much longer. They goin' to find out where I am pretty soon."

Mama walked back out in the yard carrying a pair of Uncle Earl's shoes and overalls.

"I think you can wear these, and here's five dollars," she said. "I've known your daddy for a long time, never knew him to tell a lie. Figure he taught you the same. Best thing for you to do is go down to the creek and follow it north. You'll come to the Jackson Highway Bridge. Get on the highway going north, keep going and don't come back. This is a bad place for colored, all the time."

Billy slipped the shoes on and took the overalls.

"They fit," he said. "Thank you, ma'am, I won't forget this."

"Now go on," Mama said.

"Tell Daddy I'm goin' to the Army," he said.

"I'll tell him," she said.

He took off running toward the creek.

He had just disappeared into the woods when we saw Mr. Sterling's old Model A turn down our road, with three other cars following him. He pulled up in the yard, killed the engine and got out. He was toting his shotgun.

He walked up to Mama and tipped his hat.

"Mrs. O'Rourke, Buzz. Beg your pardon but we're looking for that Johnson boy. He's done tried to take advantage of my girl Henry. Last we seen him he was comin' this way. Thought you may have seen him."

A car door squeaked and we all looked toward it. Lucas Sorenson, Sr. got out of his Ford coupe and slammed the door. He stood there, his foot on the running board with an old Colt pistol stuck in his belt. He didn't say anything, but he sure was looking around.

He was a little skinny man with steely gray eyes. He'd squeeze his eyes up like a sugar creek snake, brush his hand through his silver hair and spit his tobacco on the ground. He was always the first to join anything that was against the colored. A colored boy from down in the river land had an argument with Sorenson over a mule and turned up floating in the Mississippi with a bullet in his back. Everyone knew who did it, but no one would testify against him.

The other men stayed in their cars. When Mama looked at them they kind of lowered their heads like they weren't too proud of themselves. They just sat there, listening to the conversation.

"What you going to do with him when you catch him, Henry?" Daddy asked.

"Teach him a lesson he won't forget."

"Like what?" Mama said. "Castrate him?"

"Mrs. O'Rourke, I'm shocked that came out of your mouth."

"How do you know he did anything?" Mama said.

"Leon Moore saw him do it, and my gal said he did. That's all the proof I need."

"Well I wouldn't put much stock in that checkers player telling the truth," Mama said. "For that matter, ain't Henry been going down to the juke joints, dancing and carousing with the colored down there?"

Mr. Sterling's faced turned red. He looked at the men in the cars. They all seemed surprised at what Mama said. Even Sorenson glanced at him, but never changed his sour expression. Mr. Sterling switched hands with his shotgun, and turned back to Mama.

"That's not so, Mrs. O'Rourke. Some folks have been telling lies. My girl ain't ever been to nigger town."

"You may not know, but I know for a fact she has," Mama said.

"Forgive me, ma'am, but I think you might mind your own business."

Daddy took a couple steps toward Mr. Sterling, stopped, and eyed the shotgun in his hand.

"You speaking out of turn now, Sterling," Daddy said. "I'd hate to have to shove that shotgun where the sun don't shine."

"Now you watch your language, Buzz," Mama said. Daddy never looked at her or said anything he just kept his eyes on Mr. Sterling and the shotgun.

"Don't want no trouble with you, Buzz," Mr. Sterling said.

"You sure it's not Henry you're mad at?" Mama said.

"I'm trying to protect my girl, ma'am," Mr. Sterling said.

"Either way, Billy ain't here," Mama said. "So take yourself and the rest of your bunch and go."

"Are you sure he's not here, Mrs. O'Rourke? Maybe in the barn?"

"Mr. Sterling, are you questioning my word?"

"No ma'am, of course not."

About that time a sheriff's car turned off the road and headed toward the house. Mr. Sterling saw the car, tipped his hat, and he and Sorenson got back in their cars. The sheriff's car pulled up behind them, blocking the road, and cut the motor off. Sheriff Bowman got out, pushed his white Stetson back on his head and walked up to Mr. Sterling's car, propping his foot up on the running board.

"What are you and these other upright citizens doing here, Sterling?" Charlie asked.

"We're looking for that no-good Johnson boy. He tried to take advantage of my girl."

"I heard. That's why I came out here. His daddy called me, told me all about it, said Billy might be coming this way. It seems your girl was the one doing the dirty deed."

"Ain't so. That's just a lie. I intend to find that nigger and make him pay for messing with my girl."

"Leave the boy alone. I've never known Nate Johnson, or Billy, to lie about anything. Go on home. If there's anything to be done to Billy I'll do it, not you. Do I make myself clear, Sterling?"

"Yeah, I hear you Sheriff, but I want him to pay for it."

"I'll have a talk with Billy, tell him to stay away from Henry."

"That ain't enough, Sheriff. He needs to be taught a lesson."

"That ain't going to happen as long as I'm sheriff."

"Maybe you won't be much longer if you keep takin' them niggers' side."

"I'm not takin' sides, I'm enforcing the law. If you hurt Billy, you're going to jail. Now go on home."

Mr. Sterling sat in his car, staring at the sheriff, cranked the engine up, circled the sheriff's car, and they all left.

The sheriff turned to Daddy and stuck out his hand. "Been huntin' lately?" he said. They shook hands.

"Haven't had time, Charlie," Daddy said.

"What you goin' to do now that there's no more cotton to pick?" Charlie asked.

"Don't know. I was going to help Mama with the crop but that twister cleaned us out. I was thinking about going to Oakridge, Tennessee. They got government jobs there that pay pretty good, and it's supposed to be something that will help win the war. Since they won't take me in the Army, I thought I could make a livin' and help the war effort, too."

"That's very patriotic of you," Charlie said, "but if you would like to stay in Angel Point I could use another deputy. Bill Hastings quit to go work in Jackson and Sammy's loyal as a hound dog, and not much bigger, but he's not the brightest light in the forest. I need someone with some smarts and common sense to help me. I got a murder on my hands. The coroner said that girl your boy found was about twenty years old. She was strangled, probably raped. Wasn't much of her left. She was too decomposed to tell for sure, or even take pictures for visual identification. Most of the white folks around here don't care who she was, as long as nobody bothers their family. And that bunch who just left are goin' to cause more trouble. Small minded people do small minded things. I swore to uphold the law and that means protecting the colored, too. That's where you come in. I need someone with the guts to stand up and be counted."

"I'm not qualified to be a deputy. I didn't finish the eighth grade, I had to help Mama when Daddy died. I don't think the town's people would take too kindly to me being a deputy."

"I don't care what they think. I know I can count on you, and you can shoot a gnat's ass off at a hundred yards. Beg your pardon, ma'am," the sheriff said. Mama just shrugged.

"Plus, the job pays $37.50 a week, with a raise in six months, a car to drive, and you can get stamps to buy more than the four gallons of gasoline a week you're allotted now. I got an old .38 I'll let you pay out at two dollars a month.

84

The uniform, bullets and the badge are furnished by the county. All you have to buy is your Stetson hat. What you say?"

"Well, I do need a job. You really think I can do it?"

"Of course I do. I got a murder to solve, and that bunch out looking for Billy. It would be a lot easier if Angel Point had a police force, but they don't. I got the town and the county. I need you now."

"Okay, it's a deal. You got a new deputy."

"Good. You can start tomorrow." They shook hands. "Come by the office in the morning and I'll have the mayor swear you in. You can bring your mama and Tee for the swearing in, about ten o'clock," Charlie said.

"My Daddy's a deputy," I said. "Wow, thanks, Sheriff."

"You're welcome, Tee," he said, and grinned.

Sheriff Bowman walked over to his car and got in.

Mama waved and went back in the house.

Sheriff Bowman motioned for Daddy to come closer. Daddy stepped closer to the open window and leaned in a bit.

"Buzz, there is one thing somebody might bring up," the Sheriff said. "Earl was making white lighting before he went to the Army, and selling it out of the field in fruit jars. It wasn't much so I left him alone."

"I didn't know you knew about that," Daddy said.

"If anyone brings it up, tell them you got nothin' to say about it and it will go away."

"Far as I know," Daddy said, "he made one batch and it was so bad he didn't make anymore. I was afraid he would poison somebody. I don't think Mama knows. I would like to keep it that way."

"That's why I didn't arrest him," he said. They both laughed.

"See you in the morning, Buzz," the sheriff said. They shook hands and the Sheriff cranked his car. Daddy stepped back and waved as he turned the car around and was gone. I pretended to not have the slightest idea what they were talking about.

(16)

We arrived at the sheriff's office a little before ten. We saw Mayor Richard Blackstone's car parked in front of the sheriff's office. When we walked in, the sheriff and the mayor were waiting.

The mayor stepped up in front of Daddy and shook his hand. "Charlie tells me you want to be a deputy."

"If you'll have me," Daddy said.

"I think you will make a good one," he said, and tugged his pants up over his pudgy belly.

The mayor was around Mama's age, but short and fat. He had gray hair and a short grey beard to match. His big brown eyes ran up and down like a window shade when he talked. Daddy said he had a 'gift for gab' that wore down his opponents. He was also the school principal. Most people only voted for him because they thought he would take it out on their kids if they didn't. He did expel two high school kids last year for what he said was disobedience, but the parents had campaigned hard against him before he did.

"Mrs. O'Rourke, you hold the Bible for your son while I swear him in," the mayor said. "Tee, you can hold the badge and give it to me to pin on when I finish." We nodded as Charlie handed Mama the Bible.

After the swearing in, we went next door and ate lunch at Melba's Lunch Box.

When we walked outside after lunch, Old Man Sorenson was leaning against the café wall, his Colt stuck in his belt, a pint of whisky in his back pocket, and that meaner-than-a-rattlesnake look directed at the sheriff.

"I heard you made O'Rourke a deputy, but I had to see it to believe it. Now we got two nigger lovers as lawmen. Us white folks ain't got a chance."

"You're an evil man, Mr. Sorenson. God will reckon with you," Mama said.

"Mrs. O'Rourke," Sorenson started in, "you're another one of those misguided nigger lovers that thinks they're as good as white folks."

"You're out of line, Sorenson. Shut your mouth," Daddy said.

"Luther, you're drunk, and you can't carry a pistol in city limits," Charlie said.

"No, you sure can't," the mayor said, wagging a finger at Sorenson.

"Shut up, fat boy," Sorenson said, staring at the mayor. If looks could kill, the mayor would have been dead.

"That's it, Luther," the sheriff said. "Give me the Colt, you're going to jail."

"Mama, you and Tee get in the car," Daddy said, and we did.

"Why don't you let your new deputy do it, Sheriff?" Sorenson said, and placed his hand on the butt of the Colt. "Let's see if he has any guts."

"He doesn't have to prove anything to you," Charlie said.

"What you goin' to do if I don't go, shoot me?" Sorenson said. He looked at the crowd that had gathered, laughed, and the crowd laughed.

"Sorenson," Daddy said, above the laughter.

Sorenson turned to the sound, and Daddy jerked the Colt out of Sorenson's belt and slammed him to the ground in a split second. It looked like a bumble bee on a mosquito. He jerked the whisky out of his back pocket, tossed it away, pulled Sorenson's hands behind his back and put a knee on his neck.

"You're hurting me," Sorenson said.

"Can I borrow your cuffs, Charlie," he said. "I haven't got mine yet."

Charlie grinned, snapped the cuffs from his belt and handed them to him. He handcuffed Sorenson's hands behind his back, threw him on his shoulder like a sack of flour, and headed for the sheriff's office. I jumped out of the car and followed.

Some woman from the crowd yelled, "You could have killed that old man, O'Rourke. Why did you do that?"

"He was resisting arrest," Charlie yelled to no one in particular. "He did what I was about to do. Show's over, break it up."

Charlie caught up as Daddy entered the door and grabbed the jail keys off a hook and unlocked the nearest cell.

"Put me down, you big bastard," Sorenson yelled.

Daddy held Sorenson about three feet over one of the bunks, by his shirt and overalls, and dropped him. He bounced off the bunk like a rubber ball and hit the floor. Charlie unlocked the handcuffs and stuck them back on his belt. They walked out of the cell, leaving Sorenson on the floor. Charlie locked the cell. Daddy handed him the Colt and Charlie stuck it in his desk drawer.

Mayor Blackstone came rushing in, his face red. "What the hell you doing, Buzz! I think I made a mistake swearing you in. Sorenson could sue for excessive force."

"You damn right!" Sorenson yelled from the floor of his cell. "I think he broke my arm."

"Wasn't anything excessive about it," Charlie said. "He did what he had to do, to subdue a drunk with a gun."

"You rather he killed someone, Mayor, maybe you?" Daddy said.

The mayor's face got even redder. "I see your point, but just the same, send him home when he sobers up. I don't want any charges against him."

"Mayor, the man is a constant troublemaker," Daddy said. "He's right where he belongs."

"Just the same, do what I asked you to do," the mayor said, with a big frown on his face. He walked out, waving his arms and talking to himself.

Charlie picked up the cell keys off the desk, and hung them back on the hook. "You'll do," he said, nodding his head, a big smile on his face.

"You were great," I said.

"What're you doing here? I told you to go to the car."

"Yes sir, but you didn't say to stay in it," I said.

"Sometimes you are too smart for your own good, little man," Daddy said. Charlie laughed. Daddy couldn't help but laugh and I did, too.

Charlie patted Daddy on the shoulder. "It looks like being a sheriff's deputy is your thing, Buzz, you handled that real well. Could have been a mess if Sorenson had got that gun out of his pants. All in all a good start."

"Thanks Charlie," Daddy said.

Mama and I were real proud of him.

(17)

I was sitting on the front porch swing with the radio on, listening to Terry and The Pirates, when I saw a strange car turn off the road. It was green and had stars on the front doors and hood. Mama came to the screen door and looked out. She unlatched the screen and stepped out on the porch to get a better look. She gasped and stumbled backward and sat down on the swing beside me like her feet had been kicked out from under her. She knew something I didn't.

The car pulled up in the yard and the driver cut the motor off. I got up from the swing and moved closer to the car. He opened his door with U.S. Army painted on it and got out. He was tall with broad shoulders. He wore a funny-looking hat with a screaming eagle on it like Uncle Earl's. He was all dud-ed up in a uniform with a bunch of medals hanging off his chest and his shoes were so shiny you could see your face in them. He had a big envelope in one hand and a small blue box in the other. He stepped up on the porch and looked at Mama.

"I beg your pardon, ma'am. I am Colonel Bryan from the Department of War. Are you Mrs. Alma O'Rourke?"

"Yes sir, I am," she said, swallowing hard. "Will you be telling me something has happened to my boy?"

The man took his hat off and held out the envelope for Mama to take. When she didn't, he laid it on the swing, opened the blue box and placed it on top of the envelope.

"I'm so very sorry. Sergeant Earl Edmond O'Rourke was killed in the D-Day landing. He gave his life for his country and his comrades. The Distinguished Service Cross is in that box. That's the second highest award the country has for bravery. He was a true hero."

She never looked at the envelope or the blue box, only rocked in the swing, staring straight ahead. The colonel stood there in silence, twitching his shoulders like his uniform was itching him. As she rocked, tears clouded her eyes. She stopped swinging and stood up. Her legs gave way and she sat back down hard in the swing. She looked at me with a sadness I had never seen before. I would see it again and again in my mind for the rest of my life.

She turned back to the colonel and blurted out angrily, "What's a D-Day? I don't know army talk. What does that mean? All I know is when an army car comes calling, somebody's son has been killed. Mrs. Cox told me all about it, how an army man came and told her her son was dead. Now here you are telling me the same thing." Mama wiped her eyes with her apron. She still hadn't looked at the envelope or blue box. It was like it would somehow disappear and Uncle Earl would be okay if she didn't touch it.

The colonel sighed before speaking. "There was a massive invasion of Normandy, France on the 6th of June to try to shorten the war. They called it D-Day. Thousands of soldiers and sailors from all the Allied countries took part; many died. Your son was one of them. I'm sorry."

"When will they send my boy home?" she asked.

The colonel dropped his head, and then looked back at Mama. "I don't think he will be coming home, ma'am. His buddies buried him on the battlefield. They marked his grave with his rifle, and got his dog tags, but everything was happening so fast, and there were so many, that by the time the beach was secured most of the rifles marking the graves were gone. It was impossible to know where he was buried.

"There were plenty of witnesses that saw what he did on the battlefield. He wiped out two machine gun nests single-handedly and held the enemy at bay with their own guns while his company advanced and captured the remaining forces. There's a citation in the envelope. On behalf of the President, the U.S. Army, and myself, we are very sorry for your loss."

"I won't get to give him a Christian burial?" she said.

"You could have a memorial. The Army would send an honor guard," he said. "But to be truthful, I don't think they will ever find him."

"Were you there?"

"No ma'am. If you need to get in touch with the Army for any reason there's a phone number and information on your son in that envelope. Being Sergeant O'Rourke's beneficiary, you will get a check in about a month."

"A bene-…what?"

"It means you will receive his insurance money."

"I don't want money, I want my baby!" Mama jumped up and ran in the house.

We heard a scream and the colonel looked at me. He glanced at the blue box. "He really was a hero," he said. "Remember that. Someday it may give your family some peace."

"I think you better go," I said.

"I think you're right, son." He got back in the car and left. I picked up the blue box and the envelope and took them inside.

About an hour later, Mama opened her bedroom door. Her eyes were red and swollen. She handed me a paper with a phone number on it.

"Trenton, go up to Mr. Barnes and have him call your Daddy and tell him about Earl."

"Yes ma'am," I said, grabbed the paper and hurried out the door.

The Barnes' were always kind enough to make phone calls for us. They owned about everything that was worth owing, including the canning factory and a five-hundred-acre farm with one of only two houses near Angel Point with air conditioning, electricity and indoor plumbing. And Beau's father was the foreman, with a house with all the modern things, too.

We were farming forty acres with a five-room clapboard house, a barn and an outhouse. It was one of my chores to put a bag of lye in the outhouse hole every month to keep the smell down.

Mama was one of the best farmers ever and I didn't care what the Barnes' had, except for maybe the telephone.

(18)

Mr. Barnes was standing beside a wagon in his pin-striped overalls with the side buttons undone, to accommodate his expanding waistline, his straw hat pushed back on his sweaty forehead. His glasses were sitting halfway down his sunburned nose. He was counting watermelons.

As I walked up, he glanced my way and kept counting melons. "Are you looking for Beau?" he asked.

"Mama just found out my Uncle Earl was killed in the war. She wanted me to see if you would call Daddy at the sheriff's office and let him know."

"Sure I will. I'm so sorry. Earl was a fine boy. Let's go in the house and I'll see if I can get your father. What's the number?"

I handed him the piece of paper.

He took it and turned to one of his hired hands. "Take that load on to town. We'll pick another one when you get back."

The man nodded and climbed up on the wagon, let the brake off, snapped the reins on the horse's back and rolled away.

I followed Mr. Barnes in the house and into a big room with a fireplace that was boarded up for the summer. There were a couple deer heads and several large bass mounted on the walls. A big desk and several leather chairs sat in the middle of the room. This was my first time in an air-conditioned house. He sat down in a big high-back leather chair, picked up the phone and dialed. I heard someone say, "Hello."

"Hello, this is Allen Barnes. This Buzz?"

"Yes sir," I heard him say.

"Buzz, I don't know how else to say this other than to just say it. Your brother has been killed in the war. Your mama needs you."

"Oh my God," I heard him say. The next thing we heard was a dial tone. Mr. Barnes let the phone slip from his ear.

"I guess he's on his way," Mr. Barnes said and placed the phone back on its hook.

Mrs. Barnes walked in, huffing and puffing on her inhaler.

"I heard about Earl." She bent down and hugged my neck. She smelled like magnolias. "I'm so sorry, Tee," she said, gasping for breath.

"Now just calm down, Becky, you'll bring on an asthma attack," Mr. Barnes said.

"It's just so terrible," she said. "That makes three young men from Angel Point who've been killed in that awful war. Our son could be next."

"Yes, he could be. It takes brave men like Cody and Earl to put an end to it. Hitler and them Japs didn't give us a choice."

Mrs. Barnes shook her head and went hurrying off to another room.

We walked outside and an old Mexican man with skin like leather walked up and stood there until I thanked Mr. Barnes again and started to walk off. I slowed my pace and listened.

"I tried to get Ethan to come home," the old man said. "He was pretty drunk. He's nothing like your Air Force son Cody. He told me to mind my own business, he was a grown man and would do what he wanted. Don't think he'll come home if you don't go get him. He's down there in river town."

"I'll take care of it, Pedro. You and the boys take that load of melons to town. Don't let his mother hear about this."

"He's asking for real trouble, Mr. Barnes," the old man said. "Some folks saying he might have murdered that colored girl. They had seen him pick her up several times from those honky-tonks. People talk."

"I know. That boy's going to be the death of me."

The old man nodded and walked away. So did I.

When I got back home, Mama was sitting on the front porch swing, staring off into space. Her eyes were red, but she was making an effort for me to not see her crying.

I felt mad knowing someone like Ethan was alive and safe while Uncle Earl was dead.

(19)

Word spread fast about Uncle Earl, probably by Mrs. Barnes. People started coming by the house one after the other, bringing flowers, cards and food. Country folks feel like food is the best remedy for grief, and by nightfall we had enough to last a month. Mary Ann Simpson came by to pay her respects. She and Uncle Earl were high school sweethearts, and most everyone expected them to get married when he came home.

My parents decided they wouldn't have a memorial like the colonel suggested, but planned one of their own.

Daddy drove Uncle Earl's coupe out in the field, siphoned out the gas and took the wheels off. Mama sat his picture on the hood. Daddy poured gasoline on the car and set it afire. Mama kneeled and prayed as it burned. I sat down on the ground beside Daddy. He took a sack of Bull Durham out of his shirt pocket, rolled a cigarette and lit it .When the car fire burned out, Mama got up, wiped her hands on her apron and walked back to the house.

"It seems like the good Lord doesn't know who to take to heaven anymore," Daddy said. "First your mother, who was an angel right here on earth, and now a hero like Earl. No matter how you figure it, it ain't fair and it ain't right." He stood up, took a look at the smoldering car, dropped his cigarette on the ground and walked back to the house.

When we got back, Daddy went to his room. I saw Mama through an open door, folding a pair of Uncle Earl's pants to put in a trunk. A large jackknife fell out of the pants pocket. Mama picked it up, looked at it longingly for a moment, and motioned for me to come to her.

"Here, Trenton, take this. If it's alright with your daddy you can keep it. I know Earl was planning on giving it to you anyway."

"Thanks, Mama." I took the knife and began looking it over.

"Now be careful with it. It's real sharp," she said.

"I know. It's the one Uncle Earl used to skin squirrels and rabbits with."

Daddy walked in and saw me holding the knife.

"What're you doing with Earl's skinning knife, Tee, you want to cut your hand off? Give me that." He reached down and snatched the knife out of my hand.

"I gave it to him, Buzz. I thought he was big enough to handle it. Earl wanted him to have it," Mama said.

"Well he's not," he said, angrily. "You're too young." He stuck the knife in his pocket. "I'll be back later."

He walked out and slammed the front door. I heard his car start up and pull off. Tears ran down my cheeks as I stood there staring at the front door.

"He forgot his gun," I said through tears.

"He's not going to work, laddie."

"I'm sorry I was crying," I said.

"Don't be. He gave that knife to Earl for Christmas a few years back. He left to keep you from seeing him cry. He'll probably go to the graveyard and talk to your mother. He does that when he feels like the world's closing in on him."

"I didn't know," I said, and wiped the tears away again.

We didn't talk much about Uncle Earl after that. Daddy said it hurt too much. Mama left his burned-out car sitting in the field like a monument. She took the star out of the window, and every now and then she would walk out in the field to the old car, touch it, wipe her hands on her apron and walk back to the house.

Daddy wanted Mama to give up on the farm but she wouldn't hear any of it. She said she was going to plant a new crop and that was that. She tried to make a deal with some of the sharecroppers but there were no takers. They were either too busy or didn't want to try and start a crop in late summer.

About the time it seemed hopeless, Nate sent his brother Jesse over, and he agreed to replant because Nate asked him to help Mama. Jesse looked a lot like Nate, about the same size, but younger.

Mama asked him if they had heard from Billy and he said Nate got a letter about a week ago. He was learning how to operate a bulldozer in Alaska. He didn't get to be a paratrooper. But no matter, he was learning something useful.

"How's he doing?" Mama asked.

"He's getting weaker every day," Jesse said. Apparently, Nate needed some test to find out what was wrong with him but couldn't find a hospital in Mississippi that would perform the test on colored people.

"I'll see if Buzz can find someplace to test him."

"Thank you, ma'am. He's fading away right before our eyes," Jesse said.

"Tell him I wish him well," Mama said.

"Yes ma'am. I'll bring Homer over tomorrow and start plowing."

(20)

Daddy wouldn't let me go to town by myself anymore because of the murder, and he hardly ever had time to take me. The one Saturday he did take me to the movies the theater was almost empty. The movie we saw, "Bullets and Saddles," wasn't very good. Red Ryder was coming on later. I liked Little Beaver, but he didn't want to stay.

After the movie, we were in the car about to head home when Sheriff Bowman walked up.

"Buzz, can I see you for a minute?" he said.

"Sure, Charlie. What's going on?"

They walked to the back of the car to talk but I could still hear them.

"Buzz, the whole town's going into a panic. We have to find the killer, they're afraid he might strike again, this time on a white girl."

"It could happen if we don't come up with somebody," Daddy said.

"Vicksburg's crime lab called. They have an ID on the girl in the well. Her name is Cindila Williams. She worked as a dancer at the Apollo. The manager there said Ethan Barnes often picked her up at closing time. Everyone knew why. The question is, did he pick her up the night she was murdered.

"The crime lab said she had been in the well for maybe three or four weeks, but no one reported her missing. Ethan admitted he picked her up sometimes, but of course said he didn't kill her or dump her in the well."

"Do we need to bring him in?" Daddy said.

"Yeah, since we can prove he did pick her up at different times, that makes him a suspect. I thought we better bring him in for questioning," Charlie said. "I'll get Sammy. You take the boy on home and meet me at the office. I don't think he'll give us any trouble, but you never know. Remember that. Never trust a suspect, no matter what they say. You don't know the truth until it's done."

Daddy nodded his head and walked back to the car.

"Daddy, you think Ethan killed that girl?" I had to ask.

"You were listening, huh," he said.

"I couldn't help it."

"No, I don't think he did. He's not much, but I don't believe he would do something that bad. He was in the wrong part of town, but you're too young for me to discuss it with you." He cranked the car and we drove away.

Mr. Barnes got a high-priced lawyer from Jackson to get Ethan out of jail. Daddy said they couldn't find anything to hold him on and the judge ordered him released. The sheriff had Daddy tail Ethan everywhere he went for about a week before the Jackson lawyer found out about it and said he was going to sue the sheriff for harassment. Ethan had not been charged or convicted of anything.

With Mr. Barnes unhappy, it didn't look good for Charlie getting re-elected. If he lost, it may mean Daddy didn't have a job and we would be moving to Tennessee. To everyone's surprise, Charlie had the county newspaper publish an announcement that he was resigning effective immediately to take a job as a U.S. Marshal in Jackson. Everyone thought the real reason he quit was because of what happened with Ethan Barnes. Mr. Barnes dropped the lawsuit when Charlie quit.

Charlie recommended that Bradford O'Rourke be appointed sheriff until the general election two months away. Daddy was appointed with the support of Mr. Barnes. Sammy stayed on and the commissioners authorized another deputy.

Old Man Sorenson's boy, Luther Jr., was the only one who applied for the job. He was a security guard at the canning factory. A lot of people who didn't like Junior were upset when he was hired for the night shift.

Daddy said Junior favored his old man in the face, but that was where it ended. He was a little bigger and heavier than his old man. He had those same steely gray eyes and looked like he could hold his own in a fist fight. He was in his mid-twenties, lived alone and had never been involved with his father's bad deeds, so he deserved a chance. His mother drowned in the bathtub when he was a boy, with an empty vodka bottle sitting on the floor. There was a rumor that old man Sorenson drowned her, but nothing ever came of it.

I used to see Junior at the movies on Saturday. He would come in by himself, sit down on the back row and sleep for hours. Sometimes he would watch a movie, and sometimes he would wake up and go home in the middle of one.

He never said a word to anyone. He stayed to himself most of the time, but he did have one talent the people of Angel Point called on him for. He could find water with a willow or peach tree branch. They called it 'witching' a well. Some folks doubted it, but I saw him do it. Mr. Barnes needed a new well and Junior told him he would witch him one. Mr. Barnes said he could try, but he though witching wells was something the Indians made up. Beau and I watched him witch the well and the water was right where he said it would be, and how many feet down he said it was. Knowing Junior could do that made people think he was strange and that it might even be the work of the devil.

(21)

I was churning butter when Beau appeared from the corner of the porch, all out of breath. He put his hands on his knees and sucked in some air.

"Somebody else die?" I asked.

He straightened up and took another quick breath. "Your daddy called Mr. Barnes, and he sent me down here to tell you and you're grandma that your daddy arrested a man for the murder."

"Are you kidding me, Beau?"

"No, it's true, I swear," he said and crossed his heart. "Where's your grandma?"

"She's in the barn." I let the churn handle slide down in the butter and we took off for the barn. Mama was coming out, carrying a bucket of chicken feed.

"Mama, Beau said Mr. Barnes sent him down to tell us Daddy arrested a man for killing the colored girl."

"Is that a fact? Who is it?" she asked.

A puzzled look came on Beau's face. "I don't know...but I'll go ask!"

"It's all right, we'll ask Buzz when he comes home. Thanks for letting us know," Mama said. Beau nodded and took off running.

Mama said she thought it might be Willie Alcott. Me, I couldn't think of anyone else since Ethan wasn't a suspect anymore. Maybe things would get back to normal now and everybody would quit getting on Daddy to find the killer.

About six o'clock, we went out on the front porch, sat down in the swing, and waited for him to come home. About an hour later he pulled up in the yard, cut the motor off, got out and walked up on the porch without saying anything.

"Well," Mama said, standing up. "You going to tell us what's going on?"

"I got a suspect in jail," Daddy said. "A man from Merritt, that wide spot in the road toward Vicksburg. The cast Charlie made of the tire tracks by the well matched his tires and he had some of the same type of rope found around the girl's neck.

"Pete Markel was in town when we brought him and the truck in. He said he had seen the truck before. Said he was out partying one Saturday night a while back when he saw a truck pulling up on the road from the Foster place before midnight. He knew what time it was 'cause he had to pick up his wife from the canning factory night shift that night. He even remembered the truck had a dented front fender. He said he never paid any attention to the license plate. He may or may not be telling the truth. Pete is always four sheets to the wind.

"The suspect's name is Eddie Kendrick, a thirty-year-old white bricklayer. He's been arrested twice before for assaulting his wife, and beating up a guy at a honky-tonk. He said someone stole his truck while he was drinking at the Green Frog Club and found it the next day on the side of the road towards Vicksburg, out of gas. Someone had hotwired it.

"When I asked why he didn't report it missing he said no need, he got his truck back and he had had enough run-ins with the law. The only part that worries me is he claims his truck was stolen after midnight. If it was, he couldn't have done it if Pete's telling the truth about the time he saw it. Kendrick said he went out to jump off a friend's car about one in the morning and his truck was still there.

"But everything stays the same around here for now, Trenton. You got me?"

"Yes sir. Sure messed up my summer," I said.

"Trenton, that's cruel," Mama said. "What do you think it did to the family of that young colored girl?"

"I'm sorry," I said.

"I know," Mama said. "Now go wash up, it's almost time to eat."

(22)

After supper, I walked out on the front porch and saw a woman walking down our road toward the house, but I couldn't make out who it was at first. When she got closer, I saw it was Mrs. Sterling. I waited in the yard for her to get to the house. She walked up to me and I saw her eyes were red, like she had been crying.

"Mama, come out here," I hollered. She came hurrying out of the kitchen with a frightened look on her face.

"What is it," she said, all excited, before seeing Mrs. Sterling's tears. "My goodness." Mama opened the front door. "Come in, Mattie, what's wrong?"

"It's Henry, she's gone," she said and walked in. "She said she was going to bed about nine last night. When I went to her room to wake her this morning she wasn't there. Her bed hasn't been slept in and she's still missing. I don't know if something happened to her or if she stayed out all night. She has before. I've managed to keep it from Henry so far. I was waiting for Buzz to come home, so I could ask for help."

"You know where she would go?" Daddy asked.

111

"Probably down there in the river land to those juke joints. I don't know which one. She loves to dance. Any other time I would be furious with her, but with what's been happening in this town lately I'm scared to death something bad has happened to her. I should have let Henry put her in that reform school."

"I'll drive back to town and look for her. I think I know where she might be, I've seen her there before."

"Mattie, why don't you stay here while Buzz looks for Henry," Mama said. "Let's go in the kitchen and I'll make you some coffee." They got up and I followed along.

Later that evening, we were waiting on the front porch when Daddy drove up. Mrs. Sterling started crying again, but this time it was a happy cry. He cut the engine off, got out and opened the door for Henry. She just sat there and wouldn't get out.

"Get out of the car, Henry, and go to your Mama, now," he said. "She has been worried sick." Henry slid across the seat and got out. Her dress was dirty and her hair was tangled. Her makeup was smeared on her face and she looked tired.

Mrs. Sterling and Henry stood there staring at each other. Neither one moved. Then they broke into tears and hugged each other's neck.

"I'm sorry, Mama. Does Daddy know?"

"No, I won't tell him."

"We won't either, Mattie," Mama said.

"Where were you, child?" Mrs. Sterling asked.

Henry backed off and dropped her head. She didn't say anything. Daddy walked up to her and pushed her head up with his hand.

"I found her walking down the road toward town. She wouldn't say where she had been. You owe your Mama an explanation, girl."

Henry looked at her mama. "I drank too much and spent the night at the High Time on a couch in the back. No one bothered me."

"Oh my God," Mrs. Sterling said. She put her head in her hands and began sobbing.

"Mama, I know how disappointed you are, but Daddy hates me for being a girl. He's always telling me how much trouble girls are. He even gave me a boy's name. He said he will be glad when I'm grown, but he won't let me grow up, I can't have any friends. When I try to be good no one notices. The only place I feel wanted is in the juke joints."

"That's not true," Mrs. Sterling said. "We love you, but you can't do the things you're doing and expect us to not be upset."

"You let Daddy beat me with a belt when he couldn't find Billy, just because he was mad. He'll do it again."

"I should have stepped in and stopped it, but you were acting like one of those river land girls."

"Mattie, if I hear of Henry abusing her anymore I will have to step in," Daddy said. "The court could take her away from you. I don't want to see that happen. You two have a lot of fences to mend. I'll take you both home and you can talk some more. Henry, this is a dangerous time in Angel Point. Stay home. It's not safe to be out at night by yourself."

Henry nodded. "Don't worry, I think I've worn out my welcome there, too. I have no place else to go."

(23)

We didn't hear any more about Henry's night out and the next day Daddy took me to town to buy new shoes and overalls. We parked in front of the mercantile store and started to get out when we saw Henry and Willie Alcott standing by Tucker's Grocery. Willie was kissing her square on the lips and people were staring at them. That was something you didn't do in public in Angel Point. Henry hadn't learned anything.

"Why don't you arrest them," I said.

"If they keep it up, I'll have to, for lewd behavior," he said.

"I bet she's going to catch it when her daddy finds out," I said.

"I'm afraid Sterling is going to blame him," Daddy said. "Tee, you wait in the store and try on some shoes. I'm going to have a talk with them."

Daddy watched me go in the store, and I took a position to see the corner of the drug store through the window. The mercantile door was propped open because they didn't have air conditioning. I could hear them talking.

"Hey kids, I need to talk to you," he said.

"About what?" Henry said.

"About what you're doing in public," he said. "That's not acceptable behavior and I can take you to jail for kissing on the street. Mind you, I don't want to, but it's illegal. Besides, someone is going to tell your daddy, Henry, and he's going to be furious when he finds out. He might take it out on Willie. It's just not a good thing to do in public. You understand."

"We're not hurting anyone," Willie said.

"Yes you are. You're breaking the law and you're setting a bad example for the other kids in town, not to mention you can go to jail. Henry's under the age of consent, Willie. That could get you sent to prison."

Willie turned loose of Henry's hand and stepped back.

"My daddy don't care," Henry said.

"You know that's not true, Henry. You're already walking on thin ice. Are you going to have to get into serious trouble before you figure it out? We just had this conversation yesterday. How did you get to town, anyway?"

Henry batted her eyes and looked off in the distance.

"I picked her up," Willie said.

"Get on back to work, Willie, before you wind up in big trouble," Daddy said.

"You going to tell my daddy, Sheriff?" Henry said.

"No, but someone will, you can bet on that. I got enough to worry about without you two making a scene. Now get, Willie!"

Willie gave Daddy an evil look and stormed away.

"Wait 'til my daddy hears how you humiliated me," Henry said.

"I don't think that's a good idea. Remember what happened when you had the problem with Billy."

"It's none of your business," Henry said.

"Yes it is, Henry. I'm trying to help you. Now I understand your father's frustration. Enough is enough. You be-

have yourself, I don't want any more trouble out of you."
Daddy shook his finger at Henry and turned back toward
the mercantile.

I hurried away from the open door and started trying on
shoes again. I had been running around all summer without
any and they felt like I was putting my foot in a vise or
something. But the law said I had to wear shoes to school, or
that was what parents told us kids, anyway.

Mr. Grayson came over. He was a little skinny man about
Daddy's age, maybe five-four with a crippled left arm and
hand about half the size of his right one.

"Tee, you can't wear those," he said. "They're two sizes
too big. They will rub blisters on your feet in a hurry."

He reached up on a shelf with his good hand, picked up
a shoe box and handed it to me. "Try these," he said. I took
the box and sat down to try them on.

"How you like that motor airplane," he said.

"I love it."

"I held it for you for a month on your daddy's word he
would buy it. I knew he would. Man's word is his bond. Remember that, Tee."

"Yes sir, I will," I said as Daddy walked in.

"You get those kids straightened out, Buzz?" Grayson
said.

"I hope so," Daddy said.

"Henry is going to get some boy in serious trouble,"
Grayson said. "Looks like they would do something with
that girl. She's no good. Needs the daylights whipped out of
her. Got a demon in her or something."

"That may be why she's so defiant, beat on too much,"
Daddy said.

"Well, sooner or later she's going to get into trouble she
can't get out of, if you know what I mean," Grayson said,
nodding his head up and down.

"I hope not," Daddy said and gave me a long look. I pretended not to hear and went on looking at my new shoes.

"You like those shoes?" Daddy said, pointing at them.

"If I got to wear shoes, they're okay," I said.

"I gave him a pair that will fit," Grayson said. "He's going to need some new overalls too, right?"

"I don't know what size. Mama usually does this, but she's been feeling poorly lately."

"Hope she's okay," Grayson said.

"I think so, just kind of wore down with the new crop and all."

"Give her my best," Grayson said.

"I will, thanks," Daddy said.

Henry walked in front of the Mercantile, stopped, looked in the open door and gave us a cold stare, and walked on by.

"That girl's going to give you more trouble, Buzz, I can see it in her eyes. Got some of that Sterling in her. Holds a grudge, like her old man," Grayson said.

"Just a little mixed up, happens to a lot of teenagers, me included. I sowed some wild oats when I was a boy."

"What did you do, Daddy?" I asked.

"Nothing you need to know about. Go try on those overalls," he said.

Grayson put his good hand on my shoulder and guided me to the overalls.

"I'll tell you sometime when Buzz isn't around," he said and grinned.

"I heard that," Daddy said. "You better not, George."

Mr. Grayson rang up the shoes and overalls. "That's ten-fifty, Buzz," he said.

"Man, things keep going up, I'll have to get a part-time job to make ends meet," Daddy said.

"Yeah. This war has got everything going up. But at least most people are working, not like ten or fifteen years ago," Grayson said.

"Well, maybe Hitler and Tojo will get theirs soon," he said, and handed Mr. Grayson eleven dollars.

Mr. Grayson took the money, nodded in agreement and gave Daddy his change.

"I got to go, George. Thanks for taking care of Trenton."

"You bet. Watch out for that girl. She's a troublemaker," Grayson said.

Daddy nodded and we continued out the door.

"How is Henry a trouble maker?" I asked.

"Nothing to concern yourself with, Tee. Some people just seem to draw trouble no matter what they do, and Henry is one of them. She has a hard time realizing her actions affect other people. Or she doesn't care. Either way, the results turn out bad most of the time."

"I'm not sure I know what you mean," I said.

"You will when you get older," he said.

(24)

When we got home we couldn't find Mama. We looked all through the house but she wasn't there.

"Run out to the barn, Trenton, and see if she's there," Daddy said.

I saw her as soon as I entered the barn. She was lying on the hay by the chicken coop, a basket of eggs spilled out next to her.

I ran to her, shouting for Daddy. I dropped down and put my arm underneath her head. "Mama, what's wrong, talk to me!" Daddy came running into the barn.

"Let's get her to the house," he said and picked her up. "I better stay with her, Trenton. You run up to Mr. Barnes and tell him to call Doc Crawford."

I went flying out of the barn. That's one time I bet I could have out ran Beau.

Mama was awake and talking to Daddy when I got back. She insisted she didn't need a doctor, but she was running a high fever and too weak to get out of bed. Doc Crawford showed up about an hour later. He spent another hour examining Mama against her protest. He came out of her room and closed the door and walked over to me and Daddy.

"Buzz, your mama has double pneumonia. She should go to a hospital, but I know how hard that would be. She also has an irregular heartbeat. That will probably clear up after we get the pneumonia under control. If it doesn't, we'll find out why. If you need me, call. I know you have to work and Tee's too young to take care of her. Maybe you could get some help. I'll give her a prescription and a few samples I have of the medicine. You can pick up the prescription tomorrow after you get someone to stay with her. Try to keep her in bed and take the medicine. It could turn out bad at her age if she doesn't. Mrs. Danton may be available. Don't think she would charge much."

"Thanks, Doc, I'll call her," Daddy said.

"Well, got to go," Doc Crawford said. "The Braxton girl's about ready to domino. Better have a look at her, may be time to deliver the baby. Let me know how your mama's doing."

"Yes sir, we'll do that," Daddy said.

Doc Crawford stuck his head in Mama's room. "Alma, you stay in bed and do what your boy tells you or I'm coming back to take you to a hospital, you hear?"

"I hear you, you old sawbones," Mama said.

Doc Crawford grinned, picked up his bag and left.

"Is Mama going to be okay, Daddy?" I asked.

"We got to make her stay in bed," Daddy said. "It wouldn't hurt to use a few tears on her. I hate to resort to trickery, but your grandma is as stubborn as a Missouri mule."

"Yeah, I know," I said. "I'll take care of her."

"I'll be back in a little while. I'm going up to Mr. Barnes' to call Mrs. Danton. Keep the doors locked. Don't let anyone in. If someone tries to break in, Mama's shotgun is in the corner." I nodded and he left.

Daddy picked up Mrs. Danton the next morning and brought her to the house. She was what they called a midwife, and took care of people, including delivering babies. She was younger than Mama and maybe fifty pounds heavier. She wore overalls, short hair, and no makeup. She looked more like a man than a woman. Mama raised some cane about taking care of herself, but couldn't even get out of bed.

Mrs. Danton slept on a rollaway bed in Mama's room. Mama didn't like it too much, but Mrs. Denton was a member of our church, which helped Mama's attitude a little.

I rode to town with Daddy to get Mama's prescription. When we went in the drug store, I saw a row of flashlight bulbs sticking out of a cardboard display sign. For some reason they fascinated me. Although I didn't have a flashlight, I wanted one. When Daddy went to the back of the store to get the prescription I pulled one of the bulbs out and stuck it in my pocket. As soon as I did I knew I shouldn't have, but Daddy and Mr. Walton were looking my way as they walked back to the cash register and I couldn't put the bulb back. I walked out of the store with the bulb in my pocket. I expected Mr. Waldon to come running out of the store yelling thief, but he didn't. Daddy told me to wait in the car while he went into the telephone office. As soon as he entered the door I took the bulb out of my pocket and threw it away. I never stole anything again.

Late that afternoon the telephone man and a light company man showed up and they ran a line from the telephone pole at the road to the house. Not only did we have a phone, but we had electricity, too. Only trouble was we had to do without the electric until we could get money up to wire the house. They did install the phone, though. Mama liked to have had a heart attack when the man told her it would cost three dollars and fifty cents a month.

The telephone man called Daddy at the sheriff's office to check the phone and let me talk to him. That was the first time I ever spoke on a phone. He asked to speak to Mama and she refused, saying it cost too much and she sure wasn't paying for it. Daddy had Mrs. Danton come to the phone and told her to call him if Mama got worse, and to tell her he would pay for the phone and she shouldn't be worrying other people to use theirs.

(25)

It was a week before Mama could get out of bed. She was still moving slow but doing some of her light chores. She was feeding the chickens when we saw Nate riding Homer down the dirt road to our house. He slid off of Homer and tied him to a tree. He took off his hat and walked up to the porch. He had lost a lot of weight and looked older.

"I heard you been awful sick, Mrs. O'Rourke. Thought I better check on you."

"I heard the same thing about you. Come on in."

"Maybe I better stay out here, ma'am," he said.

"Nonsense, it's hot out there," she said.

Nate stepped up on the porch. Mama turned and pushed the screen door open and he followed her in.

I was a little surprised. White folks didn't let colored come in their house in Mississippi. They made their way to the kitchen and sat down. I went out on the back porch, and left the door open so I could be nosy.

"Would you like a glass of water, Nate?" He hesitated for a moment.

"No ma'am. How you feelin'?"

"I'm doing much better," she said. "Jesse said they weren't sure what was wrong with you."

"Yes'um. The doctor says there's something bad in my blood. I need some kind of special testing but nobody here will run the test on colored blood. Guess they think the blood'll turn black, or something." Nate smiled and Mama did, too.

"Is there some place that will test your blood?"

"I think the hospital in Jackson will, if you pay 'em a lot."

"How much?" Mama asked.

"They want a lot more for colored, maybe as much as a hundred dollars," he said. "I ain't been able to work lately. My wife works at the canning factory and Billy was helping until that thing with Mr. Sterling. By the way, thanks for watching out for my boy. I told him to come see you. You would know what to do."

"Not really. That bunch was determined to hurt him. The only thing I knew to tell him was to get out of town."

"That was the right thing to do," Nate said. "A colored boy couldn't have reasoned with a mad white man, and there was a bunch of 'em."

"Wait here, Nate," she said. Mama stood and Nate jumped up. She wiped her hands on her apron. "Sit back down, Nate, I'll be right back."

His knees began to buckle and he placed a hand on the chair to hold himself up. He saw me on the back porch looking in.

"My old legs ain't what they used to be, Tee. How you doin'?"

"Okay. I hope you get to feeling better," I said.

"Well thank you," he said.

"I sure miss going to town on Saturdays with you," I said.

"That was some good times," he said.

Mama returned. "Have a seat," she said.

126

Nate sat down, took his handkerchief out of his back pocket and wiped his sweaty forehead.

"Here's a hundred dollars," she said, holding the money out for him to take. "You get the test done."

"Oh, no ma'am. I can't take that kind of money, you need your money, too," he said.

"Nathan Johnson. How long we known each other?"

Nate seemed surprised at the question, and studied an answer for a few seconds.

"About ten years, I think," he finally said.

"Then we know each other pretty well," Mama said.

"Yes ma'am, I think so," he said.

"Then I can tell you the truth."

"Yes'um," he said.

"I got to raise a crop next spring. I don't trust anyone but you to do it. You can't if you're sick. Now take the money and I don't want to hear any more about it."

She handed him the money again and this time he took it.

"You're a true friend, Mrs. O'Rourke. I know what you're doin' and I appreciate it. You can take this out of my crop money next year."

"It's a bonus. You're the best hand I ever had. You don't owe me anything."

"I think I better go before I make a fool out of myself," he said and wiped a tear from his eyes. He got up and headed for the door, stopped and looked back at Mama. "Mrs. O'Rourke, we gonna plant the biggest and best crop ever next year." Mama nodded in agreement. I thought I saw a tear in her eye too.

He stuck the money in his pocket and walked out.

I got off my bed and went into the kitchen.

"You think he will be okay?" I asked.

"I don't know," she said, staring at the doorway. She wiped her hands on her apron and looked at me. "How would you like an apple pie?"

127

"Yes ma'am, that would be great!" I said.

"Give me about an hour and it'll be ready. I'll have to use molasses, I don't have any more sugar stamps for this month."

"Sounds okay to me," I said. I knew she was trying to do something nice for me, but she was trying to get Nate off her mind even more.

It tasted good and I ate half of it in one sitting. Daddy finished off the other half when he came home.

Daddy said Mr. Sterling and Willie had a showdown over Henry. Seems Mr. Sterling got wind of what went on in town and went after Willie with an axe handle. Mr. Sterling looked tough, but he was no match for Willie, who was ten years younger and bigger. Willie took the axe handle away from him and beat him up pretty bad with his fist. Daddy had to put both of them in jail. Mr. Sterling posted bail but Willie didn't have the money and would be there until the judge heard the case. He said that kind of worked out good, though, because neither one could get at the other.

Mama told him about Nate's visit and the money she gave him for the blood test out in Jackson.

"Sometimes I just don't understand what people are thinking, especially with someone's life at stake," Daddy said. "Just plain bad."

PART TWO
EVERYTHING CHANGES

(26)

A couple of days later I got to go to town with Daddy to get a haircut. I knew he would go by the jail and I would get to see the man he arrested. After Mr. Reynolds lowered my ears, as Daddy called it, we went to the jail. Sorenson Jr. had pulled the graveyard shift and looked like it. His eyes were half open and he had trouble getting up from the swivel chair at his desk.

"Boy, am I glad to see you, Sheriff," Luther said. "No matter how much sleep I get, I still have a hard time staying awake at that dawn hour. It's like someone is pulling a shade over my eyes."

"Yeah, I know what you mean," Daddy said. "You can go on home. Sammy will be here soon."

"Thanks," Luther said and made his exit.

Willie was sound asleep in his cell, snoring like a bull elephant, while that Eddie guy paced back and forth.

"Hey Sheriff," Eddie said. "That asshole has been snoring for hours, I can't get any sleep. And twinkle toes never got his butt out of that chair all night."

"Watch your mouth, Kendrick, my boy's here."

Eddie moved a bar space down and saw me. "Sorry, little sheriff, didn't know you was here."

Eddie looked like a nice man with wavy black hair and brown eyes. He didn't look like someone who would kill a woman.

"Wake that guy up, Sheriff. He's driving me nuts," Eddie said.

Daddy walked over to Willie's cell and ran a tin cup across the bars. The sound would wake the dead, but not Willie.

Willie turned over, stopped snoring, but never woke up.

Eddie shook his head and sat down on his cot.

I started to laugh. Daddy looked at me and I cut the laugh off.

"Are we going to get anything to eat?" Eddie asked.

"Melba will be over from the diner in a little bit with your breakfast."

"I don't get to say what I want for breakfast?" Eddie said.

"If it was up to me I would let you starve to death, Kendrick."

"I didn't kill nobody, Sheriff. Somebody hot-wired my truck. The worst thing I did was get drunk. I wouldn't hurt a lady, white or colored."

"But you don't have no qualms about beatin' up your wife," Daddy said.

"I slapped my wife once. I know I shouldn't. I told her I was sorry, but she called the law anyway."

There was a knock on the door. Daddy opened it and Melba came in, carrying a tray of food and cups of coffee for Willie and Eddie.

Melba had a pretty face with big soft cocker spaniel eyes, and long wavy brown hair, but she had been sampling her own cooking too much, and was big as a number two washtub across her back side.

"Hi Melba," Eddie said. "You fix me a good breakfast?"

"You got grits, scrambled eggs, fried bologna and biscuits like all prisoners get. Take it or leave it," she said.

"Yum, yum. I can hardly wait," Eddie said and sat down on his cot.

The smell of the food must have woke Willie. He stood up, stretched and walked over to the bars to get his breakfast.

Eddie looked at Willie. "Well, you decided to get up, Rip Van Winkle?"

"Shut up, Kendrick. I ain't talkin' to killers," Willie said.

"Yeah, well I hear you don't mind loving on a little girl," Eddie said.

"Both of you shut up," Daddy said. "Eat your breakfast, Willie. I'm going to let you out after you eat on your own recognizance," Daddy said.

"On my what?" Willie asked.

"I asked the judge about that," Daddy said. "He said it meant on your word that you would show up on your court date. I don't want to spend any more of the county's money feeding you. You stay away from Henry and Sterling or you'll be right back in here. I'll let you know when they set a court date. And don't leave town."

"I lost my appetite, Sheriff. Let me out of here." Willie said.

Daddy picked up the keys and unlocked Willie's cell. He hurried to the front door, with Melba right behind him with his food on the tray. They walked out, slammed the door and were gone.

"I'll give you my word I'll show up for court, Sheriff," Eddie said.

"That's not going to happen," Daddy said. "Sammy will be here in a few minutes to put the irons on and take you to the outhouse."

"You think I can just turn it on and off like a faucet, Sheriff?"

"That's your problem," Daddy said.

Eddie saw me staring at him. "Little sheriff," he said. "I never hurt anybody, in spite of what your daddy thinks." Eddie was looking me straight in the eye.

There was something about him that I liked. I had a feeling he was telling the truth.

The door came open and Sammy walked in. Sammy was thin and small. He kind of looked like an older Alfalfa from the Little Rascals He came up to my daddy's shoulders. His cowboy straw hat made him look a little bigger, but not what most folks thought a deputy should look like. They made jokes behind his back, but he was as tough as a ten-cent steak and didn't let his size get in the way of doing his job. He had a big gun on his hip that made him tilt slightly to the right when he walked. He was drafted but couldn't pass the physical. They discovered one leg was shorter than the other, which probably accounted for the reason he leaned with the gun. He had two brothers in the Army somewhere in Italy. He was born and raised in Angel Point. He had a girlfriend in Vicksburg, he said, but no one in Angel Point ever saw her. His daddy was the school janitor and his mom was a dressmaker.

"Sammy, I got to check on my mama, she's feeling poorly," Daddy said. "You need any help taking Kendrick to the outhouse before I go?"

"No, I can handle it. He gives me any trouble - I'll buffalo him." Sammy said.

"That pistol is big enough to do it, but I don't know if you are, Sammy," Eddie said and laughed.

"Don't you have any doubts, Kendrick. It won't be the first time the butt of this gun has banged some heads," Sammy said.

"That's enough, Sammy," Daddy said.

"He gets on my nerves," Sammy said. "I'll be glad when we get him to trial."

"Well we all know how that's going to turn out, don't we," Kendrick said and kicked his bed.

Daddy turned and looked at Eddie. "You'll get a fair trial."

"Bullshit," Kendrick said.

"What did I tell you about your mouth," Daddy said.

Sammy walked over to his desk and sat his lunchbox on the desk behind the Samuel Theodore Phillips name plate and sat down.

"I need to go to the outhouse, deputy," Eddie said.

"All right," Sammy said. "In a minute, after I drink my coffee."

"Drink your coffee after you take him out, Sammy, or it may be too late," Daddy said.

"It will," Eddie said, "and you get to clean it up, deputy."

Sammy frowned, stood up and took the cell keys off the hook and walked over to Eddie's cell and motioned for Eddie to step back. He did, and Sammy unlocked the cell door.

"Hold out your hands," Sammy said to Eddie. Again, he did what he was told.

Sammy put the handcuffs on him.

"Good thing you didn't make me put my hands behind me, deputy, you would have had an unwelcome chore," he said and grinned.

Sammy gave him a hard look, and shoved him toward the door. Daddy opened the door, Sammy followed Eddie out. A well-dressed man wearing a suit and tie stepped up on the porch.

"I come to get you out, Eddie," he said.

"I got to pee first," Eddie said. "They wait 'til you bust," and continued walking toward the outhouse.

"Sheriff O'Rourke," the man said, "my name's Navel Smith. I have been appointed as Eddie Kendrick's attorney. I have a bail bond signed by Judge Black for Eddie's release. He agrees there's not enough evidence to hold him in jail."

"Let me see it," Daddy said. He looked it over and handed it back to Smith.

"Okay, when he gets back we'll let him go, but you may be letting a killer out to do it again."

"Doing my job, Sheriff," Smith said. Sammy and Eddie came walking back from the outhouse.

"Take the cuffs off, Sammy," Daddy said. "He's got bail."

"That's wrong," Sammy said.

"Don't matter, does it," Daddy said.

Eddie held out his hands, grinning at Sammy. "Looks like you lose, little man," he said. Sammy frowned and un-cuffed him.

"He has a trial coming up. I'll let you know," Daddy said. "Make sure he don't take off."

"You're dead wrong, Sheriff," Eddie said. "I never killed nobody. Bye, little sheriff."

I started to wave but thought better of it.

Eddie and Mr. Smith stepped off the porch and Sammy walked back in the office, shaking his head.

(27)

As we walked out on the street, we saw Aunt Sara Beth get out of her DeSoto with a money bag in her hand, going into the bank. Either she didn't see us, or she didn't want to see us. It was no secret that she and Daddy didn't get along.

"It looks like your auntie is putting more money in the bank, Trenton," Daddy said.

"Have we got money in the bank?" I asked.

"Nope, and not much anywhere else, either. Get in the car, Trenton."

When we got home, Mama put supper on the table, but Daddy just pushed it away and sat there, staring at the plate for the longest, then he went outside to have a smoke. I started to go with him but Mama called me back and said to let him be.

After about an hour he came in and sat down at the table again.

"You want to eat now?" Mama asked. "I'll heat it up."

"No, I've been thinking, Mama. This town needs an experienced lawman. I don't know what made me think I could do this job in the first place. I don't have any training in law enforcement. I'm an ignorant cotton picker. I think I'll resign and take that job in Tennessee, if I can still get it. I can't prove Kendrick killed that girl." Mama wiped her hands on her apron and sat down at the table with him.

"Let a judge and jury decide that, Buzz. I know how you feel. If quitting is what you think you should do, then do it, but I can't go with you. This is my home. This is where our roots are, and it's where I'm goin' to die. You're a smart boy. I truly believe you will do the right thing."

"I wish I felt that way," he said. He gently patted Mama's hand, got up and put his hat on.

"Are you going to see Mother?" I asked.

"Yes, how did you know?" he said.

"Mama told me. She said when you had an important decision you talked to Mother about it."

"I do. It gives me peace."

"Can I go?"

"Let him go, Buzz," Mama said.

"You sure, Tee?"

"Yes."

"Okay, I hope I'm doing the right thing."

"You are," Mama said.

"Come on, Tee. Let's go have a talk with your mother."

As we pulled up to the graveyard, the first thing I saw was the preacher's grave. It still had wilted flowers all over it. Not too far from the preacher I saw Grandpa's grave. Daddy parked the car close to a big oak tree and got out. I saw her tombstone. It had Elizabeth with Liz in parenthesis, her birth date and date of death: March 22, 1940. Daddy's name was next to hers, with a blank death date, waiting.

"I loved your mother very much, Tee. She had her sights set on being a teacher before she got ill. She loved kids and everyone liked her. She would have been a good one. I miss her so much and think about her everyday."

"I do too, Daddy. I can't remember much about her. I do remember she called me into her room right before she died and said 'I love you. Find your dream and never give it up.' I'm not sure what that meant."

"You will when you're older," he said. "I'm surprised you remembered. You were five years old."

We looked at each other. We both had tears in our eyes. He reached down, took my hand and looked at the grave.

"Liz, I brought our son with me this time. I'm not as smart as you, but I'm trying to raise him the way I think you would want me to. We miss you very much. I got a real problem and I thought you might could help. Seems I may be in over my head, being a sheriff. I thought I might move on and let someone else take over."

A sudden burst of wind blew up and caught some of the preacher's flowers and blew them across three or four graves and they stopped on top of my mother's grave like that was their destination. A cold chill ran down my back. I looked at Daddy. He was staring at the flowers.

"I think I know what to do now," he said. "What your mother told you to do is what I should do. With the exception of raising you, this is the most important thing I have ever had to do in my entire life. I can't quit now." He looked at the tombstone in thought for several minutes, then spoke "You always give me the strength to go on, sweetheart," he touched the tombstone and rubbed his hand across her name.

"I'll be back to see you soon, Mother. I promise," I said.

(28)

Daddy brought books home from the library nearly every night to try and learn all he could about criminals and the law. Sometimes, we would wake up in the morning and he would be passed out at the kitchen table with an open book and a full notepad.

He was trying to solve a murder and I was trying to deal with how much I missed having a mother. Mama tried her best to take her place, but it wasn't the same. I didn't understand why. It was like Daddy said, life's not fair.

The more I thought about it, the more I felt the need to go back to the grave. But I was forbidden to leave the farm by myself and I wanted my next visit to be just me and my mother. It wasn't too far to the cemetery from our house. I considered going anyway, but I knew my mother wouldn't have approved of me disobeying my daddy.

I needed to go to town to sell a load of corn with Jesse, that helped some. Mama had twenty-five bushels stored away to sell this winter, but decided to sell it now for money to plant the new crop.

The deal was, I would ride to town with Jesse and Homer to sell the corn, collect half for Mama, give ten dollars to Jesse and have him give the rest to Nate.

I fought off the urge to go check on the movies and went to the sheriff's office. Daddy and Sammy were there. Sammy, passing time by seeing how fast he could draw his pistol, Daddy reading some kind of paper. I sat down on a bench and watched Sammy.

Daddy laid the paper down and looked up at Sammy. "You're getting on my nerves, quit drawing that thing, it might go off and shoot somebody."

"No I won't," Sammy said.

"Quit anyway," Daddy said. Sammy sat there for a second more, took his hand off the handle, picked up his coffee cup and went to get more coffee.

A tall, thin elderly man walked in, wearing pinstriped overalls, a red bandana around his neck and a Union Pacific railroad cap.

Daddy stood up. "Can I help you?"

"Yes sir. My name's Reggie Bailey," he said. "I saw the picture of Mr. Kendrick and his truck in the paper. I've seen that truck before. Thought I better tell you about it."

"Please do," Daddy said. "He's out on bail now."

"I picked up a man standing by that truck on the Vicksburg highway one Saturday night about a month ago, around two o'clock in the morning. I felt sorry for him and stopped. He said he ran out of gas and needed a ride to Vicksburg. It wasn't Kendrick, though."

"You're sure?" Daddy said.

"Yes, he was a little fellow, maybe in his twenties. Short black hair, clean-shaven, wearing Levi's and a green plaid shirt."

"A little fellow? How big?" Daddy asked.

"Well, I'm six-one," Bailey said, "so I think he was probably five-six or seven."

"That doesn't sound like Kendrick," Sammy said.

"Someone told me about the murder but I didn't connect it until I saw the picture in the paper yesterday of Kendrick and the truck. I was visiting my sick brother in Angel Point that night. I was headed back to Vicksburg when I saw him standing by that truck with his thumb out. He talked kinda funny, like one of them Yankees. I let him out on the other side of the bridge in Vicksburg. He said thanks and I drove away."

"Would you be willing to testify to that in court, Mr. Bailey?" Daddy asked.

"Sure, he was sitting right beside me. I know what he looked like."

I kept my mouth shut, but I was glad it wasn't Eddie. I liked him.

"Was there anything else you can remember about him," Daddy asked.

"He had his shirt sleeves rolled up and I saw a tattoo on his right arm. It was like a rambling bush thing. I couldn't see it too well in the dark."

"Like leaves and branches?" Daddy asked.

"Yeah, kind of like that."

"Did he say what he did for a livin', his name, anything?"

"He didn't talk much, but he could've been a farmer. He looked like he spent a lot of time in the sun, and was in good physical shape. Brown eyes, I think. His nose was a little too big for his face, with a small mouth that turned down at the corners. Kind of a permanent frown."

"That helps a lot, thanks."

"Glad to help," he said. "You think that guy could be the killer?"

"He could be. We'll have to follow it up and see what happens."

"I sure hope you catch him," Bailey said.

"So do we. Looks like you were a railroad man, Mr. Bailey."

"Over thirty years."

"Mr. Bailey, I need you to write down what you told me and we'll have it notarized to dispel any doubt about what you said. I'm going to check with the Vicksburg police and see if they have a sketch artist, if you're willing to tell them what the guy looked like."

"I can do that," Mr. Bailey said.

"Good. I'll let you know."

"I'm here a lot with my brother Norman. The doctor doesn't give him much longer. He's got pancreatic cancer."

"Sorry to hear that."

"Thank you," he said. "If you'll give me some paper I'll write out a statement for you."

"Sammy, get Mr. Bailey some paper and a pen."

After Mr. Bailey left, Daddy reread the statement. "Sammy, I'm going over to Vicksburg Monday to have a talk with the police," he said. "I may be able to get a sketch artist to draw Mr. Bailey's description of the guy. You hold down the fort Monday while I'm gone. Mr. Bailey said it was after midnight, but I don't know for sure if Pete knew the right time."

"I'll do that," Sammy said.

"Maybe the Vicksburg police can help us." Daddy said. "Come on, Tee, let's go home."

(29)

Daddy said he was going to make the rounds with the sketch of the suspect. Maybe he was a farmer like Mr. Bailey had thought.

For the next week he spent more time at the farmers' markets and tattoo parlors than the customers did and would tell me and Mama what happened. We always looked forward to hearing his latest, it was like listening to a radio show every night.

He ran across a tattoo artist who said a few weeks back he had put a heart-shaped tattoo with the name Olivia over it on the left arm of a man who looked like the suspect. He said the guy was in civilian clothes, but could have been a soldier because he wore dog tags. The man paid cash for the tattoo and never gave a name.

Daddy called Mr. Bailey before he left for work and asked him to meet at Melba's Lunch Box at noon. Mr. Bailey said he was bringing his granddaughter, so I got to tag along.

Mama had gone to the church with Mrs. Barnes to vote with the selection committee on a permanent preacher.

When Mr. Bailey came in with his granddaughter I couldn't believe what I was seeing. She was the prettiest girl I had ever seen. She had coal black hair down to her waist and shiny dark brown eyes.

They walked up to our table and Daddy invited them to sit down. They sat, she turned to me, and I froze.

"Hi," she said. "I'm Melinda Bailey. I just moved to Angel Point from Vicksburg."

For the first time ever, my mouth wouldn't work. I tried to speak but nothing came out. After a long pause, Daddy spoke. "Tee, she's asking you a question," he said.

I tried again. "I'm Trenton O'Rourke. I'll be in the fifth grade when school starts," I finally said.

"Me too," she said and smiled.

"I guess I'll see you at school," I said.

"Maybe we will be in the same class," she said.

"I hope so," I said before I thought. "I mean, that would be good. I could show you around."

Mr. Bailey put his arm around Melinda. "This is my pride and joy. My son is in the Army. I'm staying with my daughter-in-law while he's gone. We thought it would save a lot of time and money if we moved in with my brother."

"Welcome to Angel Point," Daddy said.

"Thank you," Mr. Bailey said. "What did you want to see me about, Sheriff?"

"I wanted to ask you a question and I thought it might be better if we discussed it in person. I think I have another lead on the man you picked up, and it would help if you could confirm it. Do you remember seeing a chain around his neck? Like a dog tag? Did he say anything about the Army."

Bailey looked up at the ceiling, then the floor, in thought. "You know, I don't remember him saying anything about

146

the Army. Didn't notice a dog tag around his neck, either. I'm sorry I don't remember."

"Well, thanks for coming in. Let's have lunch. I'm buying, check out the menu."

"That's very kind of you, Sheriff," Mr. Bailey said.

"That's the least I can do for all your help." He motioned for Melba to come over. "What do you want, Tee?" Daddy asked.

I couldn't take my eyes off Melinda and sat there without answering.

"Tee, you hear me?" he said.

His tone shook me out of my trance. "No, what did you say?"

"What do you want to eat?"

"A hamburger and a Coke," I said, my gaze still fixed on Melinda. Her eyes were like a magnet. I couldn't stop staring at her. I was making a fool of myself.

Fortunately, Melba showed up to take our order, and everyone's attention was directed to her instead of me.

After lunch, we said our goodbyes to the Baileys and headed for the church. We rode along in silence for a few miles before Daddy spoke.

"Kind of smitten with Melinda, weren't you, boy. She's awful pretty."

"She's alright for a girl," I said.

"From the way you were looking at her, I would say you thought she was more than alright," he said.

"Can we talk about something else," I said.

"I didn't mean to embarrass you," he said. We pulled into the church driveway and Mama was standing by the front door, talking to Mrs. Barnes.

On the way home, Mama said they wanted to hire a young preacher, but they were all in the war. They decided to hire Reverend Paul Benson from Alpine, a little town between Vicksburg and Jackson. He was in his sixties and retired, but decided he wanted to preach again. There really wasn't much choice, she said, he was the only applicant.

Mama asked how the meeting with Mr. Bailey went. Daddy told her Bailey wasn't sure, but he thought he was a soldier and was going to pursue it with the Army in Vicksburg. He didn't mention Melinda or my fascination with her, thank goodness.

I looked at him and smiled and he smiled back. It was our little secret. I was a little surprised at myself for having so much interest in a girl. On the other hand, it seemed like it was the thing to do. I wasn't quite sure why. Except what I heard a couple of older boys at school talking about confused me. I wasn't ready for girls at ten years old.

(30)

The next day, I was still thinking about Melinda, but what I was more interested in was going fishing, and wondered where Beau was. Before I could give it another thought, I looked up and saw him running at about three-quarter speed down the road. Someone probably sent him, because he only came down the road when he was a messenger, and cut through the pasture when he was on his own. I never knew why.

I waited for him to get to the house. "What's going on, Beau?" I said. "You want to go fishing?"

"We're going to be moving," Beau said. "My Daddy got a job with a big plantation in Columbia, South Carolina His brother works there."

"When?" I asked.

"Next couple weeks, I think. He got a notice on when he goes to court. Daddy said after the court thing is settled, it's time to move on. I won't ever see you again."

"We can write to each other," I said.

"You're my best friend. I'm going to miss you," Beau said and a tear fell on his cheek.

It happened to me, too, and I wiped a tear away. "Maybe you could stay with us instead of going to South Carolina?"

"He wouldn't let me, and I would miss everyone too much."

"Yeah, I know. I would if it was me. I was going to ask you to go fishing, but I don't think I want to go now."

"Me neither," he said. "I may never go fishing again. It's no fun without you."

"That goes for me, too," I said. "What about flying the airplane. Want to do that?"

"If you do," he said, and wiped another tear from his eye.

"I'll get it. I got a little gas left. I'll be right back."

I ran to the back porch, dropped to my knees by the bed and pulled the airplane out from under the bed.

"What're you doing, Trenton?" Mama asked.

"Beau's outside. We're going to fly the airplane. He said they're going to be moving to South Carolina soon. I'm sure going to miss him."

"Is he sure?" Mama asked.

"Yes ma'am. He said his daddy got a job there and they're leaving after Mr. Sterling settles with the court."

"Well I'll be. I'll have to talk with Mattie about this," Mama said.

"Yes ma'am. We'll be out in the pasture," I said.

"Okay, don't go far."

I picked up my airplane and a small bottle of gasoline, along with an eye dropper, and took off back outside.

"Here," I said, handing him the airplane. "You can fill it up."

"I like airplanes, "Beau said. "I think I want to be a pilot when I grow up."

"Have you ever been in an airplane?" I asked.

"No, but I know I would like it," he said.

"I haven't thought much about what I want to be," I said. "My mother said find your dream. I don't know what that would be. Maybe when I get older I'll know."

"When I become a pilot I can fly here in no time to see you," Beau said.

"That'll be ten years from now. I probably won't be here either, unless I decide to be a sheriff like Daddy."

"Yeah, no telling where we'll be by then," Beau said. "Maybe in the Army, if the war's not over. I bet they would let me fly an airplane."

"Let's hope it don't last that long," I said. "Give the propeller a spin."

Flying the airplane wasn't much fun. I couldn't stop thinking about Beau leaving, and as much as he liked airplanes, I don't think he was having any fun either. We didn't say anything, but after a few minutes we sat the airplane down and started talking about the things that happened to us that summer. Right at the top of our list was finding the dead body in the well.

"I don't think I'll ever forget looking in that well and seeing those big eyes staring back at me," I said. "It scared me to death. I hope Daddy finds whoever killed her."

"Me too, and what about the catfish," he said.

"It wasn't right to shoot him," I said.

"If you say so," Beau said and laughed.

"I'll always remember you, Beau. You may be gone but you will always be my best friend."

"That's the way I feel," he said. "Maybe we can write to each other like you said and meet again when we get older."

"Yeah, that would be great," I said.

"Well, I guess I better get back to the house," he said. "Daddy said he needs me to help pack everything up so we can be ready to leave. He said he thought he would get a fine, but no jail time. I hope he's right."

"Maybe Daddy could put in a good word for him, after all, he was just trying to protect Henry."

"Maybe not anymore," he said. "Henry said she's not going and if she doesn't, he's going to have to put her in reform school. There's no other place for her to go."

"I'm sorry, Beau. I wish there was something I could do to help." I looked down at the airplane and made one of the hardest decisions I ever made.

"Beau, I want you to have the airplane. Take it with you, fly it, and pretend I'm there with you."

"No, I couldn't take your airplane. Besides, your daddy would be madder than an old wet hen."

"No he wouldn't, he would understand. He gave it to me. It's my airplane and I want you to have it."

"I can't, Tee. It's your favorite thing."

"It was, but it won't be anymore 'cause all I'll do is think about you wanting to fly airplanes. Take it, and dream about flying one yourself."

"I love it, but, are you sure?"

"I'm sure, here," I said and handed him the airplane.

"I'll take good care of it," he said. He began to cry. I tried not to cry, but we both sat down on the ground and bawled our eyes out.

Beau got up, hugged my neck, and picked up the airplane. "I'll keep it always," he said.

That's what I had told Daddy when he gave it to me, I thought.

"I don't know what you're going to be when you grow up," he said, "but I'm going to be a pilot."

"I believe you," I said. "I don't know what I'm going to do, if I make it to a man."

"What do you mean by that," he asked, looking puzzled.

"Oh nothing, just talking," I said. I didn't tell him I was thinking Daddy may kill me for giving that airplane away after all he went through to get it.

He smiled, and stuck out his hand for me to shake. This time he didn't spit on it. We shook hands like men, and he walked away with the airplane. I headed for the house, working on a speech for Daddy. I was having second thoughts about giving Beau the airplane. I might pay for it on my back side.

(31)

Mama was hanging clothes when I got home. I tried to walk on by so she wouldn't notice I didn't have the airplane, but she did.

"Where's your airplane, Trenton?"

I gave her a blank stare. "Where's your plane," she asked again.

"I gave it to Beau."

"Why did you do that?" she asked.

"It was a kind of a going away present. He loves airplanes and I figured it would be better off with him than me."

"Well that's very considerate, but don't you think you should have asked your daddy about it first?"

"Yes ma'am, I guess I should have, but it seemed the right thing to do at the time. You think he'll be mad?"

"I don't think so, maybe disappointed that you didn't talk to him first."

"I'll tell him when he comes home tonight," I said.

"Kind of closing the barn door after the horse is out, ain't it," she said.

"Yes ma'am. I should have talked to him first."

"I wouldn't worry about it," she said. "I called Mattie and she said it was true they are moving away as soon as they can. Giving Beau the airplane was a nice thing to do."

"You used the phone?"

"You don't think I know how to use a telephone?"

"Yes ma'am, I mean no ma'am. I don't know what I mean. I never saw you use it before."

"Well I did, and we had a good long talk," she said. "Mr. Sterling is going to get a big raise on the tobacco farm, but she's worried about her kids. Beau is heartbroken and Henry refuses to go. They don't know what to do with her."

"Beau said they were going to put her in that reform school."

"I suppose they could do that, she's underage. I hope that don't happen, though."

"Could we let her stay with us," I said.

"I don't think so. I couldn't handle her. If I was you, I would be thinking more about what to tell Buzz when he gets home."

I sat on the porch and rehearsed what I was going to say, over and over. At a little past six that evening, I saw Daddy's car turn off on our road and I began to sweat. He pulled up by the porch and got out.

"Hi, Tee, what you been doin'?"

"Did you know the Sterlings are moving," I said.

"No, where did you hear that?"

"From Beau, and Mama talked to Mrs. Sterling. They're going to move to South Carolina as soon as Mr. Sterling gets his court stuff out of the way. I'll never see Beau again."

"Sorry to hear that. I know how close you are."

"Yes sir. That's why I need to tell you about something I did." I backed up a little and swallowed hard. "I gave Beau my airplane. You can spank me if you want to."

"I'm not going to spank you, but I am surprised. Don't you think we should have talked about it first? What if his daddy won't let him keep it?"

"Yes sir. I never thought about that. He said he was going to be a pilot when he grew up and I did it before I thought."

"Well, it's your airplane. If that's what you want to do, it's okay. In fact, I'm proud of you for caring enough to give it to him. If Sterling says anything I'll take care of it."

I think I took my first good breath since I did it. "Thanks for understanding. I love you."

"I love you, too, Tee. You're a good son."

I didn't know Mama had walked up behind me, and when I turned around she had a big smile and a tear in her eye. Something you didn't see much of from her.

"I'm proud of both of you," she said. "Your supper's ready."

After supper I went out on the front porch, ran an extension cord out on the porch, and plugged in the electric radio Daddy bought me and listened to Sky King. I didn't have to buy batteries anymore.

Mama came out on the porch and sat down beside me and wiped her hands on her apron. "Laddie, I been thinking. You have always wanted a puppy. After we tell your Daddy, we'll go to town and see if they've got one at the farm supply store. Would you like that?"

"You think he'll let me have a puppy? A real one?"

"Yes, a real one," she said.

"I want a boy, like Rin Tin Tin."

"Okay, if they have one. He's yours to take care of, mind you."

"You think Daddy will be alright with that?"

"Sure he will," she said and smiled. "My farm."

"How come you changed your mind about the puppy?" I asked.

"You're older now and can handle the responsibility. He'll be a good companion for you when Beau leaves."

"I don't know what to say, Mama, except thank you. I'm going to name him Laddie for you."

"I like it," she said and wiped her hands on her apron.

"Okay," I said. I wanted a puppy, but I knew it was about more than the dog. She was a smart lady.

(32)

Daddy came in looking tired. He took off his pistol belt, stuck it on top of the china cabinet and sat down at the kitchen table. Mama brought him his supper.

"Find out anything?" she asked.

"Naw, same old stuff," he said.

"Let it go for now," Mama said. "Trenton's got something to ask you."

"What? You give away something else?"

"No-," I started. "Mama, you tell him. It was your idea."

"What are you two cooking up?" he asked.

"I told Trenton he could have a puppy if it was okay with you."

"You're both full of surprises. You wouldn't let me and Earl have a dog, now you're helping Tee get one. I'm a little hurt."

"You can have a puppy, too," Mama teased.

"I've gotten over it," he said. "Why the change of heart?"

"He's a lot more responsible than you and Earl were at that age."

"Is that right?" he said. "Are you going to let the puppy come in the house?"

"Just on the back porch with Trenton," Mama said.

"I knew there was a catch. Where are we going to get this new family member?"

"At the farm supply store," I said. "They always have puppies."

"I guess that would be okay," he said.

"When can we get him?" I asked.

"Tell you what," he said, "I have to go by the office in the morning before I go to Vicksburg. You come with me and we'll go to the store and see if they have a puppy. I'll run you back to the house before I go to Vicksburg."

"Thank you. I'll take good care of him, I promise!"

I had a hard time sleeping that night, thinking about the puppy. The next morning we took off for the farm supply store. I spotted him the minute we walked in. He looked like Rin Tin Tin, except his fur was red. We walked back to the cages, he saw me and twisted his head. He was the one.

Mr. Simpson appeared from the other side of the cages. He was a big barrel-chested man in his fifties, with blue eyes, thin brown hair and ham hocks for hands. He looked like he could pick up a horse if he wanted to. His family had owned the store forever, and Uncle Earl and his daughter Mary Ann had been sweet on each other since they were little. She was the homecoming queen when they graduated from high school.

"Hi Sheriff, Tee," he said. "You need a puppy?"

"Don't know that we need one, but Mama said Tee could have one, so here we are. You mostly do as you're told with a woman."

"Yep, I've been married thirty years," Mr. Simpson said.

"We came to get a puppy, Jerry, but there's something else." Daddy reached in his pocket and took out a small black box. "Mama found this in Earl's things and asked me to give it to Mary Ann. It's an engagement ring. I knew he was going to ask her to marry him but we didn't know he had the ring. It was in his chest of drawers. She's free to do whatever she wants to with it. Earl would have wanted her to have it."

"That's very kind of you, Buzz, but she's not here. She moved to Jackson after Earl was killed. She said she needed to get out of Angel Point. But I'll see she gets it. Earl was a fine boy. I would have been proud to have him as my son-in-law."

"Thank you, Jerry. I know how she feels. I've considered leaving myself," Daddy said.

"Maybe we better get back to talking about puppies," Mr. Simpson said.

"I think so," Daddy said.

"I've got a litter of five black-and-tan hounds, and that mix you're looking at," Mr. Simpson said. "Which one you want?"

"The red one's got a little longer hair but he kinda looks like Rin Tin Tin," I said.

"He may be part German Shepherd. I think he's going to look like one, except for the color. I was asking two bucks for him. Roy Brown traded him to me for two sacks of mule feed, but considering you're almost family, I'll give him to you."

"You sure that's the one you want, Tee?" Daddy said. "A hound would make a good hunting dog. I don't know what you can do with that one."

"He's the only one I want," I said.

"Okay, Jerry, we'll take him. I want to pay you for him."

"No, I don't want the money. He's yours, Tee," Mr. Simpson said. "Remember, if you want to train him, the best way to do it is teach him one thing at a time until he's got it, then move on to the next thing."

"Yes sir, I'll do that," I said. I opened the cage, reached in and lifted him out. He licked me in the face and peed on me.

"Well that's a good start," Daddy said, watching the pee run down my shirt. Mr. Simpson handed me a towel.

I carried my puppy to the car. Daddy got in, cranked the car, and started backing up. The puppy jumped out of my arms and into Daddy's lap. The car was moving backwards and he was trying to get the dog out of his lap. Suddenly, a crash from behind rocked the car. Daddy put his foot on the brake and handed me the puppy.

"Hold on to him. Look what he made me do! You stay in the car." He cut the engine off and got out. I saw a very pretty lady with long blonde hair and bright red lips get out of her car. He took of his hat as he approached her. "You okay?" he asked.

"Yes, I'm fine. It's my fault," she said. "I didn't realize you were moving."

"No, it's my fault. My son just got a new puppy and it jumped in my lap as I started backing up. He distracted me for a moment and I didn't see you in time. I'm very sorry. I'll be happy to pay for any damages."

She glanced down at the cars, then looked at his badge. "I don't think there's any damage, Sheriff, you just bumped it." She stuck out her hand "My name's Paula North. I just moved to town, I'm a new teacher. Maybe you can tell me where I can find a good house or apartment to rent?"

"I'm Buzz O'Rourke. Sorry, don't know of any. Is your family with you?"

"It's just me. My husband was killed in the war."

"Sorry to hear that. I lost a brother at Normandy."

"Maybe this awful war will be over soon," she said.

"I hope so," he said. "Where are you staying now?"

"I rented a room above Mr. Tucker's store for the time being."

"I'll look around, see what I can find," he said.

"Thanks," she said. "Don't worry about the car."

"Nice meeting you, Mrs. North. I wish it had been under better circumstances."

"It's nice to meet you, too," she said. "I better go. I have a meeting with the principal."

"If there's anything I can do for you, let me know," he said.

"I will," she said, climbed back in her car, backed up, then pulled around us and was gone.

He got back in the car and started it up.

"I saw the way you were looking at that new teacher," I said. "Kind of smitten yourself, ain't you."

"So you heard?"

"Sure did," I said.

"Just hold on to that dog, young man."

(33)

Mama was washing the breakfast dishes and I was drying when we heard a car pull up in front of the house. We weren't expecting anyone.

When we got to the front porch we saw Nate's wife Princess and Jesse get out of a Model A. We knew something had happened to Nate. Mama started wiping her hands on her apron.

They walked up to the porch. She was a lot younger than Nate, but overweight with a puffy face, so she looked older. She held an envelope in her hand.

"Mrs. O'Rourke, I come to tell you my husband passed this morning," she said.

"Oh no," Mama said. "I'm so sorry to hear that." Her eyes filled up with tears. "He was a good man. I'm going to miss him very much. Would you like to come in?"

"We'll just stay out here, ma'am," Jesse said. "We're going to have the funeral Thursday morning at the Faith Temple in the river area. It's alright if you don't come, we understand."

"We'll be there," Mama said.

"That would make Nate happy," Princess said.

"Did they find out what he died of?" Mama asked.

"The doctor thinks it was sickle cell, that's mostly a colored disease that's passed down in the family. He needed more tests to be sure, but if it was, the doctor said he lived a lot longer than most."

"Is there anything I can do?" Mama said.

"I think Billy's coming. Maybe you can tell your son to watch out for us when Billy gets here," Princes said.

"I'll do that," Mama said.

"Nate had me write a note for you yesterday," Princess said. "I think he knew the time had come. I wanted to deliver it personally." She handed Mama the envelope. Mama opened it, took out the note and a hundred dollar bill fell out and floated to the ground.

Princess picked it up and handed it to her. Mama unfolded the note.

Mrs. O'Rourke,
Sorry I can't plant your crop for you.
Jesse promised me he would do it. I hope that's okay.
Thank you for the money but it was already too late.
God bless you and your family for all your kindness.
Nate

Mama wiped her eyes with her apron.

"Here," she said, "take this hundred back to help with the funeral."

"Thank you, ma'am," Princess said, "but that would be against Nate's wishes. He wanted you to have the money."

Mama nodded and put the money in her apron pocket.

"I'm sure going to miss Nate," I said. "He was my friend."

"He thought a lot of you, too," Princess said.

"I'll be here next spring to plant your crop, Mrs. O'Rourke. Don't you worry," Jesse said.

"Thank you Jesse," Mama said.

"Well, I guess we will go," Princess said. "You're welcome to come to the funeral, Mrs. O'Rourke, but if you don't it's okay."

"We owe it to Nate," Mama said. "I have to."

"Then, we will see you Thursday morning," Princess said.

"Goodbye ma'am, Mr. Tee," Jesse said, and they got back in the car and drove away.

Thursday morning Mama put on her funeral dress. I got my new overalls on and squeezed into my new shoes. Daddy started to put on his one and only suit, changed his mind, and put on his sheriff stuff in case anyone needed a reminder that this was not the time to cause trouble. So far no one had seen Billy.

The Faith Temple was across the street from the colored school. There were cars and wagons everywhere, just like at the preacher's funeral. I made the decision on the way there I would look at Nate.

Jesse was standing at the door, inviting people in. Daddy put his pistol in the glove compartment and locked it. We got out and walked in. They had all the windows raised and four ceiling fans blowing on the pews, but it was still hot. Billy was standing by his daddy's casket in his Army uniform. Princess was sitting in a front row pew with her other four kids.

I didn't know most of the people there, although I had seen some of them many times at the wagon yard. We were the only white people there. Daddy shook hands with several people he knew and we walked by the casket. I looked at Nate. He looked like he was sleeping. Princess got up and hugged Mama's neck and shook daddy's hand.

"Thank you for coming," she said. "Nate would be very pleased."

We sat down in the fourth row pew behind the family members. A tall, dark-skinned man, wearing a black suit and blue tie, came over and introduced himself.

"Thank you for coming," he said, and patted his sweaty face with a white handkerchief. "I'm Reverend Vander Tisdale from Vicksburg. Princess is a cousin of mine and asked me to preach Nate's funeral."

"I'm Buzz O'Rourke. This is my mother, Alma, and my son Trenton."

"It's nice to meet you," he said.

"I thought I would look official with the badge, in case anyone wanted to start trouble," Daddy said.

"Thank you, I heard about the trouble Billy had. I hope that's over," he said.

"Those kind of people never get over it, reverend," Mama said.

"Yes ma'am, I know what you mean," the reverend said. "It's time to start the services. Thanks again for coming." He shook hands again with Daddy and made his way back to the pulpit.

The reverend had everyone turn to 'Just As I Am' in the hymn book and sing. Four or five songs later he stepped behind the pulpit and started preaching Nate's funeral. After about twenty minutes into the sermon, the congregation rose to their feet and began shouting hallelujah and clapping their hands. They got louder and the preacher got louder, until the walls were vibrating. We sat there watching, feeling out of place.

Princess got up and ran to the coffin and kissed Nate. I had seen the kissing thing before. She cried and screamed. Billy came over to calm her down. She collapsed to the floor and Billy picked her up and placed her on the front pew. The shouting and crying was still going on. Doctor Stevens stuck something under her nose and she woke up. Billy put his arms around her, and the other kids squeezed in to hold on to their mother.

The congregation began dancing around the coffin, some crying others screaming "praise God, praise God." This went on for several minutes. We stood up, not knowing what else to do. Reverend Tisdale held up his hands and motioned for everyone to sit down. He held his outstretched arms over his head until everyone was seated, including us. He placed his hands on the pulpit and scanned the congregation with a serious gaze. There was complete silence except for the humming of the ceiling fan blades.

"It's time to send Nathan Johnson on to the Lord," he said. "If you would like to pay your final respects to Nathan before you depart, the family would appreciate it." We all stood up and walked by the coffin and then out of the church.

The funeral lasted less than an hour but it was an experience I never forgot.

We were backing the car out to leave when Billy ran up to the driver's side.

"Sorry I didn't get time to talk to you, Mr. O'Rourke. I wanted to tell you I'll be leaving in the morning. I gotta go back to the Army."

"Sterling holds a grudge, Billy," Daddy said. "He's convinced you were trying to take advantage of Henry. That other bunch of no-goods don't care as long as you're colored. You're never going to convince them otherwise."

"I'll be leaving on a Greyhound in the morning at nine o'clock," Billy said.

"Okay if I pick you up, and take you to the bus station?"

"Yes sir. Don't want you to have no trouble because of me."

"I'll pick you up at eight thirty, at your daddy's house."

Billy nodded and turned to Mama. "Thank you, Mrs. O'Rourke, for helping me when I was in trouble. I won't be running away anymore."

"It was the right thing to do," Mama said. "I knew you was tellin' the truth."

"Yes'um," Billy said. "See you in the morning, Mr. Buzz," he said. He put his army hat on and walked away.

The only thing I ever learned about what happened at the bus station was Mr. Sterling and old man Sorenson showed up, and Daddy reminded them he would take them back to jail if they caused any trouble. Billy got on the Greyhound, went to the back of the bus, and that was the end of it.

(34)

Saturday morning when he was off, Daddy got up early and fixed his famous Spanish egg omelet, as he called it. When he did that he was in a good mood with something on his mind. The last time he did he took me to Vicksburg to see a circus. Mama and I didn't like it near as much as he did. We just pretended we did so we wouldn't hurt his feelings. After breakfast he walked around the kitchen, whistling. He was really in a good mood. After half an hour of whistling we couldn't take it any longer.

"Okay, Buzz, what're you up to. You're too happy," Mama said.

"I knew you would be down after Nate's funeral and I thought I would try to cheer you up a little."

"An omelet won't do it. Out with it," Mama said and wiped her hands on her apron.

"I thought we would go to the movies this evening," he said.

"Why," Mama said. "Miss Paula going?"

"Well, yes, but I wanted us all to go," he said.

"That's what I figured. I don't want to go," she said.

That was no surprise to me. She couldn't sit still long enough to watch a movie and most of them she wouldn't have liked anyway. The few times we did get her to go she was either upset with the kissing or the shooting.

"You want to go, Tee?" he asked.

"What's on?"

"Buck Privates, with Abbott and Costello," he said.

"They're funny," I said.

"I can call Mrs. Bailey and see if Melinda can go," he said.

"Well, I have been wanting to see it, but Melinda doesn't have to go."

"It would be more fun if she went, wouldn't it?" he said.

"I guess so," I said.

"Mama, you sure you don't won't to go? It's a comedy," he said.

"No, you know I don't like to go to movies. I have some sewing to do and Mattie is coming down to show me some new cloth she bought.

"Okay, I'll call Mrs. Bailey and see if Melinda can go with us, Tee."

"Maybe Mrs. Bailey would like to go," Mama said and smiled.

"I'll ask her. Maybe Reggie wants to go, too, I'll take everybody," he said, big-eyed.

"I changed my mind," I said. "I think I'll stay home with Mama and listen to the radio."

"You and Melinda can sit by yourself," he said.

"Okay, maybe I will go. I've got my own money." They didn't know it was my drug store singing money.

"How about you pay for all of us?" he laughed.

"I don't have that much," I said.

"Okay," Daddy said. "I'll pay our way in and you can buy Melinda something."

I nodded in agreement. He picked up the phone and called Mrs. Bailey. She said Melinda could go but Reggie was supposed to help her with some canning today, so it would just be Melinda.

We picked up Melinda and then Miss Paula that evening and headed for the theater. When we arrived there was a long line. As we stood in line, I wanted to say something interesting to Melinda but was tongue tied. I couldn't think of anything to say except to ask her if she wanted some popcorn and a Coke. I bought the snacks and we followed Daddy and Miss Paula to a seat. They sat down and Melinda and I sat down in seats behind them.

The movie came on and we sat there like two tomatoes. She dropped her hand on mine and I almost peed my pants. I couldn't have moved my hand if the theater had been on fire. We watched the movie and laughed. Halfway through the movie I got the courage to turn my hand over and take hers. She looked at me and smiled.

When the movie was over we walked out into the lobby. I noticed a movie poster with a pretty black-haired girl and a horse on it. We stopped to look at the poster. The title was "National Velvet." Melinda was younger but she looked a lot like the girl on the poster. The movie was scheduled to open Christmas Day.

Daddy saw us looking at the poster. "I got an idea," he said. "How about we all get together on Christmas and come see "National Velvet" and then have supper at Melba's."

"I'd like that," Miss Paula said.

"Would you like to do that, Melinda?" he asked.

"Yes sir," she said.

"Good," he said. "Melinda, you ask your mama and grandpa to come and I'll hog tie my mama and bring her. Tee, you can bring Laddie if you like and he can sit in the lobby like he always does when you go to the movies. We'll include everyone and make it a special Christmas, and bring presents. Maybe the war will be over and we can celebrate even more."

"Sounds like a lot of fun, Buzz, good idea," Miss Paula said.

He didn't fool me. I knew he was trying to impress Mrs. North. I wish I could have thought of something to impress Melinda.

That night was one of my most memorable for a lot of reasons. I think that's when I knew Melinda was the one and I was sure Daddy felt the same about Paula North.

But as it turned out, we didn't get together for that Christmas like we planned. Too many things prevented it.

I was never able to go see the movie. It was too much of a reminder of other things that happened later, but that night was great.

Daddy and I had a talk about Miss Paula sometime later. He said he was thinking about asking her to marry him but was afraid I would resent her because of my mother. I didn't. I liked her. I was sure my mother would have wanted him to be happy. I still had a lot to learn about life, but I knew no one liked to be alone.

(35)

Mr. Sterling's trial was set for 10 A.M. Monday morning. Beau was going so I asked Daddy if I could go, too, because it was something that would be educational. I don't think he bought it, but I got to go.

The courthouse was an old red brick building, in the same block as the Sherriff's Office and Melba's Lunch Box. As we walked in, the hardwood floors squeaked and moaned like they were in pain. There was a sign above a door down the hall on the left that read 31st Municipal Court.

The courtroom had twelve chairs with a fence around them. There was a big tall desk, two long tables with chairs and five rows of church pews. Mr. Sterling, his wife and Beau walked in. A man in a uniform I didn't recognize appeared from a door behind the tall desk and motioned for Mr. Sterling to sit down at one of the long tables. Mrs. Sterling and Beau sat down in the same pew as us. Beau waved and I waved back. The man in the uniform faced us and said "All rise. The Honorable Chester V. Monroe presiding."

We stood up, and a little man wearing a black robe with white hair, a fat face and beady brown eyes walked in and climbed some steps up to a chair behind the tall desk and sat down.

"Be seated," he said and we all sat down.

"Is the defendant present?" the judge asked.

Mr. Sterling stood up. "Yes sir, I am Henry Alexander Sterling."

The man in the uniform walked over to Mr. Sterling and held out a Bible and Mr. Sterling put his hand on it.

"Do you solemnly swear to tell the truth, the whole truth and nothing but the truth, so help you God?"

"I do," Mr. Sterling said.

The judge nodded. "Is the arresting officer present?"

Daddy stood up, hat in hand. "Yes, Your Honor. Sheriff Bradford O'Rourke."

The judge nodded. "Do you have a lawyer, Mr. Sterling?"

"I do not, Your Honor."

"How do you plead, Mr. Sterling?"

"Not guilty."

"You may present your defense, Mr. Sterling," the judge said.

"I was protecting my teenage daughter from a grown man that had already tried to seduce her," he said. "I didn't want it to happen again."

I thought it sounded pretty good.

"That's not a good enough excuse for attacking Mr. Alcott with an axe handle. You could have been charged with assault with a deadly weapon and faced a felony charge," the judge said. "You should have contacted the sheriff."

"The sheriff knew about the incident before I did, Your Honor, and did nothing," Mr. Sterling said.

The judge looked at the man in the uniform.

"Bailiff, you do not have to put the sheriff under oath at this time, but I would like an answer. Mrs. Smith, please take

down his response." The woman with a funny-looking type-
writer nodded and put her fingers on the keys.

"Sheriff, did you know his daughter was under age?" the
judge said.

"Yes, Your Honor. But at the time, I thought it was better
to warn Willie and send them home."

"Mr. Alcott should have been arrested for contributing to
the delinquency of a minor. You need to bring yourself up to
speed if you are going to continue to be a lawman," the
judge said.

"Yes, Your Honor," he said. "Should I arrest him now?"

"No," the judge said. "Due to the time frame, I will address that with Mr. Alcott when he appears before me."

I thought this was going to be a trial for Mr. Sterling but
it was turning out to be one for Daddy, too. I felt sorry for
him. I think he was embarrassed. I knew how hard he studied to learn the law.

"Is your daughter going to testify, Mr. Sterling?" the
judge said.

"No, Your Honor, she refused to come."

"Then we all agree that the incident in question did happen and it may be necessary to appoint a social worker to
look into your daughter's emotional status, Mr. Sterling, but
that doesn't mean you can take the law into your own hands
and do bodily harm to another person when he has not at-
tacked you. I sentence you to thirty days in jail and a fifty
dollar fine."

Daddy stood up. "Your Honor, may I address the court?"

"You may," the judge said.

"I ask that Mr. Sterling's jail sentence be revoked because
he needs to leave Angel Point to take a job in South Carolina,
and the jail sentence could cost him the job. I also believe it is
in the best interest of all concerned that Mr. Sterling leave
Angel Point as soon as possible."

The judge looked at Mr. Sterling.

"Will you leave Angel Point as soon as possible, Mr. Sterling?"

"Yes, Your Honor."

"I won't vacate the sentence," the judge said, "but I will cut it to two weeks, and will consider reducing it to time served after a week if there is no more trouble. Sheriff, you may escort Mr. Sterling to jail. Court is adjourned," he rapped his gavel on the desk and stood up.

"All rise," the bailiff said, and the judge disappeared out the back door.

Daddy placed handcuffs on Mr. Sterling and we all walked to the jail. Daddy took the cuffs off and locked him in a cell. Mrs. Sterling and Beau came over to the cell.

"I was afraid this would happen," Mr. Sterling said. "That's way I asked Ethan to drive us here. Mattie, you and Beau go on home with Ethan. See if you can find Henry. No telling where she is. Maybe I'll be out of here in a week, thanks to Buzz."

"I'll let him call you if he needs anything, Mattie," Daddy said.

"Thank you," she said.

"Hey Tee," Beau said.

"I got a new puppy," I said. "You want to come see him?"

"I'll ask Mama if I can," Beau said.

"You can play with him. He looks like Rin Tin Tin except he's red."

"Okay," Beau said.

"Let's go, Beau, Ethan's waiting in the car," Mrs. Sterling said and they left. I was glad I didn't have to ride home with him.

Mr. Sterling walked up to the bars and wrapped his hands around them.

"I know we've never been good friends, Buzz, but the boys have, and I think we could have been, too, if it wasn't for the niggers. The ones around here don't know their place. They think they're as good as white folks, and you don't do anything to stop it."

"Henry, it's about what's right and what's not. Nobody should have to be a slave or bow down to another human being because of their color. There are good people and bad people of all colors and races. I'm sorry you don't understand that."

"Well, I guess we'll never agree on that, but thanks anyway for trying to help."

"You're welcome. If you could get Henry to go I think she would be better off someplace else."

"I've done everything I know to do for the girl," Mr. Sterling said. "I think there's a demon or something in her."

"That's too bad," Daddy said.

It had crossed my mind a few times about who had the best daddy, me or Beau. After today there wasn't any more doubt. I knew I did.

Sammy walked in, tilting to the right, and sat down at his desk.

"I know you got to take Tee home, Sheriff, I'll watch Sterling."

"He's okay. We got him for at least a week. I told Henry he could call his wife if he needed anything. Let him call. I'll be back as soon as I can. Let's go, son."

When we walked outside we saw Willie Alcott leaving Tucker's Grocery, carrying two large suitcases.

"What's he doing?" I asked.

"No telling. I hope he's not trying to leave town. Stay here, Tee, I'll be right back."

Daddy caught up with Willie. "Where you going, Willie?" he asked. "You can't leave town 'til your trial."

"I'm going to move to the Bluebird Boarding House."

"You sure they got a room?" Daddy said.

"They always got a room. I'm tired of Tucker asking me to do stuff and not getting paid for it because he gives me a room."

"Okay, make sure you show up for court."

"I will," he said.

"All right, see you later."

As we got in the car we saw Willie going into the Blue-bird Boarding House, hanging on to the suitcases. It seemed kind of funny he would move now after living at Tucker's for so long, chores or not.

"That's odd," Daddy said. "Mr. Tucker always treated Willie like he was his son instead of a hired hand. Something else is going on here."

"What?" I said.

"I don't know, but he doesn't have the money for room and board at the Bluebird. I'll pay him a visit later. I need to get you and Mama home now." He cranked the car and we pulled away.

(36)

When we got home Beau was already there sitting on the front porch steps.

Daddy drove up in front of the porch, stopped and waited for me to get out. "I've got to go back to town," he said. "Tell Mama to look for me when she sees me coming. You might better feed that dog."

"Yes sir," I said, and got out of the car.

"Where's the puppy?" Beau asked.

"I locked him up in the barn. We'll go get him. Mama doesn't want him in the house when I'm not here," I said.

Mama walked out on the porch. "That dog has been howling his head off ever since you left. I checked on him, he was alright, but he won't shut up."

"I'll go get him. Me and Beau want to play with him."

We headed for the barn. When we went in he ran to me and started licking my hand. "What did you name him?" Beau asked.

"Laddie, for my grandma."

"He does look a little like Rin Tin Tin like you said, Tee, but I never seen a red German Shepherd."

"I don't think he's full blood, but that's okay, I like him," I said.

"He's real pretty," Beau said. "I wish I had a puppy."

"We'll you can't have this one," I said. "I'm going to teach him to do all the things Rin Tin Tin does in the movies."

"If I wasn't going away I would help you train him."

"Are you leaving as soon as your daddy gets out of jail?"

"Maybe. Henry's missing, her clothes are gone. Mama thinks she's run away."

"I hope nothing bad has happened to her," I said.

"Mama said she wasn't going anywhere until she found her."

"Where would she go?" I asked.

"I don't know," Beau said. "I don't want to think about it anymore right now. Let's play with the puppy."

We let Laddie out of the barn and the first thing he did was start chasing one of Mama's Rhode Island red hens. Laddie was nipping at her and she was cackling like he was killing her. Mama came out in the yard.

"Trenton, catch that dog. I can't have him chasing the hens. They won't lay."

I made a lunge at Laddie but missed. Beau caught up with him and picked him up.

"Thanks, Beau. Let's take him on the back porch where he can't get out and I'll feed him."

"The first thing you're going to have to teach that pup is he can't chase my chickens, or he goes back to the store," Mama said and walked back in the house.

"How you going to teach him, Tee?"

"I don't know yet, but I will."

For some reason I keep thinking about Henry. There was something about the clothes thing that was bothering me. All of sudden I had it.

"Beau, I think I know where Henry is. I saw Willie with two suitcase when we were in town, going to the Bluebird. I don't think he has that many clothes. I'll have Mama call Daddy and tell him. Come with me."

I found Mama in the kitchen. "Mama, Henry has run away and I think I know where she is," I said.

"Where's that?" she asked.

"At the Bluebird Boarding House. When we were in town we saw Willie carrying two suitcases. He said he was moving to the Bluebird, but Henry's clothes are missing, and one of those suitcases may be hers."

"I'll call Buzz," she said. She dialed the number and Daddy answered.

"Trenton's got something to tell you," Mama said, and handed me the phone.

"Daddy, Henry's missing and all her clothes are gone. She may be with Willie at the Bluebird."

"You're right. I checked on Willie and found Henry there, too. I put Willie in jail for contributing to the delinquency of a minor, like the judge said. Willie said they were planning on running away to get married. I have Henry at Melba's waiting for Ethan to bring Mrs. Sterling to pick her up. That was good thinking, son. Thank you."

"I'll tell Beau," I said.

"Good, you do that," he said and hung up.

I returned to the back porch. Beau was cuddling Laddie.

"Beau, Daddy found Henry with Willie Alcott. Daddy's waiting for your mama to come get her. Ethan is going to take her to get Henry."

Beau was silent for a moment and wiped a tear away. "I feel better now," he said.

Laddie had the bed sheet on the floor, chewing on it. Mama would have had a fit if she saw him.

We took Laddie out in the woods and had a great time playing with him that afternoon. Beau never mentioned Henry.

When he got ready to go home he pulled out his all-purpose ten-tool pocket knife and handed it to me. "Here," he said. "I want you to have this." I knew it was his favorite thing. He was always bragging about how it could do everything.

"I've got a knife. Don't you think you should keep it?" I said.

"It's something to remember me by, like the airplane you gave me. But if you don't want it, I'll keep it," he said.

"No, it's not that. I always liked it," I said.

"It's yours then. I have to go home."

"Maybe you can get a puppy when you get to South Carolina," I said.

"Maybe. So long, Tee," he said and took off running.

"Bye Beau!" I yelled. He kept running, threw up his arm and waved.

I knew that would be the last time I would see him.

Mrs. Sterling picked up Henry and two days later the judge let Mr. Sterling out of jail. They left town with Henry, but without saying goodbye.

Willie Alcott's draft notice came in after he was locked up and the judge let him go to the Army instead of jail, bad eyes and all. No one in Angel Point ever saw or heard from Willie or Henry again.

(37)

We were on our way to school to register me for next year when Daddy said he had to stop by his office to check on Luther. He had been going to sleep on the job too much. Luther was sound asleep when we walked in. It took shaking his chair to wake him up.

"Luther, I don't know what the answer is," Daddy said, "but you're going to have to stay awake and do your job."

Luther yawned and blinked his eyes. "I'll do better," he said.

"You have to," Daddy said. "Now go on home."

Sammy came in a few minutes later and we headed for the school. With Beau gone I was kind of looking forward to going back to school. I knew Melinda would be there and I was getting more interested in girls lately.

When we walked in the schoolhouse we saw Miss Paula sitting at a table with a FIFTH GRADE – MRS. NORTH sign. She was going to be my homeroom teacher. We walked up to the table and Daddy took off his hat.

"Hello Sheriff," she said, then looked at me and smiled. "Are you in the fifth grade?"

"Yes ma'am," I said. "My names Trenton, but everybody calls me Tee."

"Okay, Tee, you can pick up your books. I need you to fill out a form, Sheriff. School starts the Tuesday after Labor Day," she said and handed him the form and a fountain pen.

I noticed Daddy couldn't get the smile off his face as he stared at Mrs. North. "Did you find a place to live, Mrs. North?" he asked her.

"Yes I did. It's the old Jordan place across the street from the school."

"I had forgotten about that," Daddy said.

She handed me my books and the one on top was an arithmetic book. It made me think of Beau.

Daddy gave her back the form, a smile still glued on his face.

"We're going to have a parent's meeting at the school this Friday," she said. "We would like for you to come, Sheriff."

"I think I can make it," he said without hesitation.

"Good, I'll see you Friday," she said.

A pretty dark-haired young woman wearing a blue cotton dress approached us. She was holding a little girl's hand.

"Excuse me, Sheriff," she said. "My name's Wanda Rosen and this is my daughter Gloria, she's eight years old. I work the night shift at the canning factory and my husband is in the war. She has to stay with my mother at night and I walk home early in the morning alone. I'm skeered to death for all of us. Are you goin' to catch that sicko what killed that girl, he might kill us, too."

His smile was gone. Before he could answer, two more women standing nearby overheard and moved closer. "What are you doing to catch him?" one of the women said. "We deserve to know," the other added.

"I am doing everything I can," he said.

"Well that's not good enough," Mrs. Rosen said. "We need a real sheriff."

"I can understand your feelings," he said. "I may have him soon if the FBI can identify fingerprints I sent them. I believe he may be a soldier stationed at the Vicksburg Prison Camp."

"If he's still there," Mrs. Rosen said.

Several more parents moved in. He was surrounded. Mrs. North stood up and walked over to Mrs. Rosen.

"I know how frustrated you are," Mrs. North said. "But this is not the place to discuss it. We have people waiting to register their kids and you're blocking them from doing that."

"You're new here," Mrs. Rosen said. "You don't know what we been goin' through."

"You're right, I don't. But the sheriff said he may know who it is soon. Give him a chance to do that. Why don't you go now, Sheriff, so we can get on with our job."

"Yes ma'am," he said. "I apologize for the interruption." He looked at the people surrounding him. "I will catch him, I promise." He looked back at Mrs. North. "Thank you, ma'am. I don't think I will be able to make that meeting after all."

"I understand," she said.

We turned around to leave and Mr. Bailey and Melinda were standing behind us.

"You'll get him, Sheriff," Mr. Bailey said.

"I hope so," Daddy said.

I moved closer to Melinda and she smiled.

"Let's go, Tee. We'll see you later," Daddy said.

"See ya," Mr. Bailey said.

I turned back and looked at Melinda as we went out the door. Somehow she knew, looked my way and waved. I waved back and we headed home.

(38)

It was six A.M. when the telephone rang. We had just woke up and I was still half asleep. I was beginning to think it might not have been a good idea to get a phone. Laddie was asleep under the covers.

I heard Daddy say "Hello" then, "Say that again, Doc?" After a couple of minutes Daddy said, "I'll be there as soon as I can. Tell the coroner to leave everything like it is until I get there." He hung up the phone and walked into the kitchen and plopped down at the table. He had a strange look on his face.

"Something bad has happened," he said.

"What's going on, Buzz," Mama asked.

"That was Doc Crawford. He said a milkman found Old Man Sorenson dead in his car a couple of blocks from his house this morning. He had been shot. He didn't have his Colt. Doc Crawford said he called Luther several times but didn't get an answer."

"It's hard to feel sympathy for a man like that," Mama said, "but we are all God's children."

"One of the colored probably had all they could take from him," Daddy said.

Daddy got dressed and called Luther. The telephone rang and rang but there was no answer. "He's asleep again. I'm going to have to fire him, but I can't do it now."

"Maybe he's with his daddy," Mama said.

"Maybe," he said.

"You want some breakfast?" Mama asked.

"No, I got to get to town and sort this out."

He dressed, strapped on his .38, picked up his Stetson and headed for the door.

When he opened the door we heard a car engine and saw lights hit the front of the house.

We all walked out on the porch and waited for the car to pull up.

"Who could that be this time of morning," Mama said.

"It's Luther," Daddy said, shielding his eyes from the light. "He must have found out what happened to his daddy."

Luther pulled the car up in the yard, cut it off and got out. His eyes were big as saucers and he had blood on his shirt. He walked up to the porch and stopped in front of Daddy.

"What happened to you?" Daddy asked.

"I did it. I killed him," Luther said. "Here's my gun. I shot him four times. I started to run, but I knew they would catch me. I thought it would be better if I turned myself in." He held the gun out and Daddy took it.

"You killed your Daddy?"

"He murdered my mother. I knew it, but he never said he did until last night. I just snapped and it happened. He came to the jail last night about supper time and wanted me to arrest a colored boy he said stole some money from his car while he was eating at Melba's. He said he saw him in the car and was trying to let the law handle it. The boy was about ten years old. He said he was playing in the car, pretending he was driving it. He didn't have any money on him. I told my daddy he was just a kid, and I couldn't arrest him. He went into a rage, jerked that Colt out of his belt and pointed it at the kid. I told him to put it away and he started cussing me and the kid. I was afraid he was going to shoot us both.

"He said I was like my mother, I didn't have any back-bone. That's why he got rid of her and should have done the same thing to me. Before I knew it, I pulled my gun and shot him four times. The kid took off running. My dad dropped his gun and grabbed me, his blood dripping on my shirt. I pushed him away and he staggered to his car and got in. I stood there frozen in place as he drove away. When I got my senses about me I followed him. I found him dead in the car a few blocks away. I've been driving around all night, trying to decide what to do." He dropped to his knees and started crying.

"I'm sorry, Luther, but I got to take you to jail," Daddy said. He helped Luther to his feet, put handcuffs on him, and sat him down in the backseat of the car.

"You want me to drive my car back to the jail?" Luther asked.

"No, I can't let you do that, "Daddy said, and drove off with Luther handcuffed in the back seat.

Mama and I stood there in shock, watching Daddy's car until it was out of sight.

By noon everyone in Angel Point knew what happened to Old Man Sorenson, and most were happy about it. The district attorney had Luther transferred to Jackson two days later to stand trial because he said the victim was so disliked they couldn't get an unbiased trial in Angel Point.

Luther Sorenson Sr. was cremated and his ashes thrown in the Mississippi River to prevent vandalism of his grave.

They never did find his Colt. Six months later they ac-quitted Junior of the murder, and then he moved away.

(39)

On Friday, Daddy took me and Mama to town to buy groceries. It was payday, plus he said he wanted to get her out of the house for a bit. Mama didn't go to town very often.

He dropped us off at Tucker's Grocery while he went to the sheriff's office. When we went in the store, Ray Jones was working the counter. We had seen him at church and his daddy farmed and helped out at the sheriff's office when they needed an extra deputy. He was younger, wasn't as big as Willie, and didn't look as tough. Mrs. Gates was buying some bread and salt meat there.

"Hello Mrs. O'Rourke, Tee," she said. "I haven't seen you in a while."

"We don't get out much during the summer," Mama said.

"You ready for school to start, Tee?" Mrs. Gates said.

"Yes ma'am," I said.

"Well, got to go. Good to see you again, Mrs. O'Rourke," she said. "I'll see you in school, Tee."

"Yes ma'am," I said. I thought about Henry and the reform school. That's probably what Henry needed. Didn't hurt Mrs. Gates none.

"What can I do for you, Mrs. O'Rourke?" Ray said.

"Need a few things," she said. "Here's the list. I think I got enough stamps for everything." She handed him the list and he got a basket.

"I'll get it for you, ma'am," he said and pushed the basket down the grocery aisle, picking up things on the list. I think I liked him better than Willie.

Mrs. North came in, saw us and walked over. "Hi Tee. This must be your grandma," she said.

"Yes ma'am," I said.

"Mrs. O'Rourke, I'm Paula North. I'll be Tee's teacher this coming year. I'm pleased to meet you. I wish you could have gone to the movie with us the other night."

"Maybe next time," Mama said.

Fat chance, I thought. Daddy walked in. He was pleasantly surprised to see Mrs. North there.

"Hello Paula," he said. "I see you have met my mama."

"Yes, I was about to invite all of you to dinner after church tomorrow."

Daddy smiled and looked at Mama. "What do think, Mama, can we make it?"

"I think so," she said to my surprise.

"Okay," Mrs. North said. "How about going straight to my house after church and we can get acquainted, Mrs. O'Rourke, while I fix it."

"That will be fine, Paula," Mama said. "My name's Alma."

"Great," Paula said.

Ray walked up with the basket. "Excuse me," he said. "I think I got everything, Mrs. O'Rourke. You got a few stamps left. We didn't have the five-pound bag of sugar but I gave you three two-pound ones and didn't pull a stamp for the extra pound."

"Thank you, Ray," Mama said.

"You want to put this on your bill, or pay for it?" he said.

"We'll pay for it," she said.

"Okay, I'll sack it up," Ray said. "I'll be with you in a moment, Mrs. North."

"That's okay, I'm in no hurry," she said.

It didn't look like Daddy was in a hurry to leave, either.

Ray sacked the groceries. Mama paid him. We said goodbye to Mrs. North and headed home.

"Well, looks like she got you back in church. This is getting better and better," Mama said. "That's more than I could do."

"Now Mama, don't start on me," he said.

"I'm not starting on anything. I'm just glad you're going to go to church."

"It wouldn't hurt if you would be nice to her," he said. "She lost her husband in the war and doesn't have any other family. This was the only place that offered her a job. She moved down here from Colorado to get a new start and put her grief behind her. I know you can understand that."

"I don't have any problem being nice to her. I like her."

"Me too," I said.

"Good," Daddy said. "We'll have dinner with her."

"What's she going to cook?" I said.

"It doesn't matter, Tee," he said.

"It does to me," I said.

Daddy shook his head and we rode home in silence.

(40)

That evening we heard a car pull up followed by a knock on the door. We were getting a little gun shy; every time someone came to the house it was bad news.

Much to our surprise it was Aunt Sara Beth. She hadn't been to Mama's house since my mother died. She had on her usual diamonds and her hair was dyed red like mine. She reminded me of that movie star, Rita Haworth. She was just as pretty, but that was it.

"What brings you out here, Sara Beth? You lost?" Daddy said.

She paused before she spoke. "I guess I had that coming. I knew you didn't want me coming around, and it seemed better to leave it that way until now. I need to talk to you. It's important. May I come in?"

"No," I said.

Mama stepped in front of me. "Trenton, mind your manners. That's your aunt. Come in, Sara Beth, and have a seat."

"Why are you here?" Daddy asked. "I don't think we have anything you would want."

"I came to offer you something," she said. "I heard about Luther Jr. and I know you have problems with your job. With Luther doing what he did, it may be the last straw."

"That's my problem," he said.

"Yes it is. I have been watching from afar until now. If you don't get reelected you may take Trenton away, and he may not get the chance my sister wanted him to have. I want to make sure he does."

"We do just fine," I said.

"Keep quiet, Trenton," Daddy said. "I don't know what you got in mind, Sara. I do know you wanted to have Liz cremated because you thought I was going to ask you for money to bury her."

"I was greedy and stupid," she said. "I've changed."

"How's that?" Daddy asked.

"I finally realized money alone doesn't make you happy unless you do something good with it. And I owe it to my sister to make amends."

"In what way?" he said.

"I want you to come manage the candy factory. I'll pay you twice what you make as a sheriff and give you twenty percent of the business after five years. I will also pay for Trenton's education for whatever he wants to do. I will put it all in writing."

We all looked at each other in shock. Daddy stood there staring at Aunt Sara Beth for the longest. "Is this some kind of cruel joke?" he finally said.

"No, I'm serious. I have always respected your honesty and hard work. I know you would bring that to the factory, regardless of your personal feelings. If you still want to be sheriff you can wait until the election to decide. If you don't want the deal I'll still pay for Trenton's education."

"Don't do it, Daddy, I don't want you working for her!"

"Didn't I tell you to be quiet?" he said.

"I know you will be someone I can depend on to do a good job," Aunt Sara Beth said.

"Why now?" he said.

"Because it's time I did the right thing."

"We don't need your charity, Sara," he said.

"It's not charity, it's a business deal. I need someone I can trust to run the factory."

"Considering the past, I don't know whether to believe you or not," Daddy said. "I need time for it all to sink in."

"Think it over," she said and stood up.

"I will," Daddy said. "But I promised I would find the killer, and I intend to do that."

"I hope you do," Aunt Sara Beth said. "I have to go. Goodbye, Mrs. O'Rourke. I'm sorry I upset you, Trenton. Take your time, Buzz. Let me know when you're ready."

Daddy opened the door for her and she made her way out to her car and drove off.

We all sat down at the kitchen table. "What do you think?" Daddy asked Mama.

"I never did trust that woman," Mama said.

"Me neither," I said.

"I don't know what to think," he said. "Maybe she has a guilty conscience, or maybe she's playing mind games with us."

"It's your decision," Mama said and wiped her hands on her apron. "Personally, I don't think it'll work."

"Like you said, it's my decision. I need some more time to think about it."

(41)

I woke up about six the next morning, put Laddie out and started getting dressed in my new overalls for church. I expected Mama to be in the kitchen fixing breakfast but she wasn't. Her bedroom door was closed and I didn't hear any noise in her room. I couldn't remember a Sunday that Mama wasn't up by now, getting ready for church. I knocked on her door and she said come in. When I went in she was still in bed. She didn't look right. She was pale and droopy-eyed.

"Are we going to church, Mama?"

"Not this Sunday, baby, I don't feel too good. I know your Daddy's disappointed but I'm just too tired. I told him you two should go, but he said we could make it another time and he called Paula to apologize."

"Is it all right if I fix me some oats?"

"You go on back to the kitchen. I'll get dressed," she said. "I'll feel better once I move around a little."

"Yes ma'am," I said. I looked out the window and saw Daddy out in the pasture, leaning on the hood of Uncle

Earl's burned out Ford, smoking a cigarette. Laddie was chasing grasshoppers.

I walked out to the car. "Mama up?" he asked.

"Just now," I answered.

"I can't remember when she last missed church," he said. "I told her we would go with her and we didn't have to go to Paula's but she said she didn't feel like it."

"She don't look too good," I said.

"That's why I thought it best if we stayed home. Let's go on back to the house and check on her."

Mama was in the kitchen fixing breakfast when we got back to the house. Daddy put on some coffee and walked out in the yard to have another smoke. I took Daddy a cup of coffee outside and we sat down on the porch steps. Laddie came running up and sat down beside me. Mama came to the door a few minutes later and said our breakfast was ready.

We got up and went back to the kitchen and there were two plates of pancakes and a bottle of syrup on the table, but Mama wasn't there. I went to her room and she was sitting in her rocker, reading the Bible.

"You okay, Mama?" I said.

"Yes, I'm fine. Since we didn't go to church I thought I would read some scriptures. After you and your Daddy eat, take care of the dishes for me."

"Yes ma'am," I said. "Want me to bring your breakfast to you?"

"I'm not hungry, maybe later. Go eat your pancakes."

I went back to the kitchen and sat down at the table.

"Your grandma okay?"

"She says she is but I don't think so."

"We'll keep a close eye on her. Eat your breakfast."

"I'm not hungry," I said.

"Me neither," he said. He walked down the hall and peeked in the open door to Mama's room, turned around and walked back to the kitchen.

"She's sitting in her rocker with her Bible in her lap, sound asleep," he said.

"She hasn't been acting like herself for two or three days now," I said.

"Give me the washcloth. I'll wash, you dry," he said. "She don't come around soon, we'll call the doctor. You can give Laddie the pancakes."

"Yes sir," I said and picked up the plates.

After we washed and put away the dishes, I was out in the yard teaching Laddie to grab my toy gun out of my hand like Rin Tin Tin did in the movies when I saw Sammy's car turn off the highway on the dirt road to the house. We had more visitors in the last week than in the past year. Sammy's car came to a stop in the yard. He cut the engine off and got out, holding a big brown envelope.

Daddy walked out on the front porch and waited for Sammy to step up on the porch. "What're you doing out here, Sammy?" he asked.

"We got it," he said. "I went by the office to pick up my lunch and this was sticking out of the mail box. Clyde must have delivered it Saturday. When I didn't see ya'll at church I figured you would be home, so I came on out. I'll let you open it."

"The FBI fingerprint report?" Daddy asked.

"Yes, open it," Sammy said impatiently. He handed the envelope to Daddy. He ripped the flap off. A single page was inside.

"Read it out loud, Buzz," Sammy said.

Daddy looked down at the paper and read it out loud.

To: Sheriff Bradford O'Rourke - Angel Point, Mississippi
The fingerprints you sent have been identified as those of PFC Gerald Eugene Morris. Army I363031. 133rd US Army Infantry Brigade. Company C. Vicksburg, Mississippi.

Contact command for further access to PFC Morris.

"We got him, Buzz," Sammy said.

"Maybe, let's keep this between us until I check it out."

"We can't let this guy get away," Sammy said.

"We have to go through the Army. I'll get dressed and meet you at the office in an hour. I'll try to get a warrant if I can find the judge. We'll go to Vicksburg and get him."

Sammy nodded. We walked outside with him. He got in his car and drove away.

When we went back in the house Mama was up ironing clothes.

"How you feel?" Daddy asked.

"I'm okay," she said. "I been a little extra tired the last few days. Old age I guess. I heard you talking to Sammy. Be careful. Don't take any chances."

"I won't," he said.

She picked up the clothes and headed for her bedroom.

Daddy put his hat on and bent down to look at me. "Tee, take care of your grandma while I go get this guy."

"Yes sir, I will. I love you, Daddy."

"I love you too, son. Don't worry, the Army will help me."

"Yes sir," I said. I tried in vain to stop a tear from falling on my cheek.

"It's going to be okay," he said and walked out the door.

I went to Mama's room and stopped at the open door. She was sitting in her rocking chair, reading the bible.

"You okay, Mama?"

"I'm fine, baby, go listen to your radio shows. Your dad will be back soon."

"Yes ma'am," I said and went to the back porch and turned on the radio. They had some kind of broadcast about American soldiers moving into Paris, France and how the French were so glad to see them. Maybe the war would be over soon. The Thin Man came on later but I couldn't get my mind on it so I turned it off. I tried to go to sleep on the swing but couldn't. I lay there thinking about my daddy He was in a kind of war, too, and didn't have anyone to help him. He had to come up with a murderer before it happened again. People would keep hounding him. Maybe we should have went to Tennessee. Things would have been a lot calmer.

Daddy came home a couple of hours later. He sat down at the kitchen table, took off his hat and sailed it across the kitchen against the wall and slammed the table with his fist.

"It wasn't him. A friend of his said he was with Morris in Angel Point until after midnight, and left him at the Green Frog to go home with a girlfriend around one. I found several more soldiers who said he was there after midnight and Morris has shipped out for Germany. If Pete's right, then Kendrick is right, and I'm totally wrong about everything It's time for me to resign."

"That's up to you. Maybe Pete was wrong about the time. It won't do any good to lose your temper," Mama said.

"Sorry for that." He walked over and picked up his hat, put it on and sat back down at the table.

"If you trust yourself and the Lord it will all work out," Mama said.

Daddy looked at me and Mama but didn't say anything, just shrugged his head no. He still didn't say anything. I thought of something to get his mind off it.

"Daddy, would you take me up to the Barnes' to get Beau's address? I wanted to write to him," I said.

"Sure," he said. "I need to do something right. I think Beau would like to hear from you."

When we pulled into the Barnes' driveway, Daddy asked one of his hands where Mr. Barnes was and he said he was in the barn. We drove down to the barn and got out. The doors were open.

Mr. Barnes was inside the barn, un-harnessing one of his mules.

"Be right there," he said and continued un-harnessing the mule and led him to a stall. There was a horse or mule in four of the stalls. An old black Dodge pickup was parked in the last stall with a tarp covering it. The wind had blown the tarp off the front of the truck. It had a dented right front fender. A roll of weaved rope was hanging on a nail on a post next to the truck. We were walking toward it when Mr. Barnes walked up beside us and we stopped.

"Hi sheriff," Mr. Barnes said. "What can I do for you?"

"You want to wipe that mule down before we talk?" Daddy said. "I can wait."

"Naw, he's okay. I'll do it after you leave," he said.

"We won't be long. My boy was wondering if the Sterlings left a forwarding address. He wanted to write to Beau."

"No, Henry said he thought it best that he sever any ties to Angel Point and start over. I don't even know the company he went to work for, it's somewhere around Columbia, I think. He was mainly concerned about the girl. Two-to-one she ran away again."

"That old Dodge truck run?" Daddy said.

"Yeah, only time we ever use it is for the fertilizer. Ethan takes it in to Simpson's with the boys to load, but it sits here the rest of the time. You need to borrow it?"

"No, I was just wondering."

"Would you and the boy like to come in for a cold drink?"

"Thanks, but we need to go," Daddy said.

"If I hear anything I'll let you know," Mr. Barnes said.

Daddy nodded and we got back in the car and left.

As we pulled up into the front yard, Daddy stopped the car, cut it off and sat staring out the windshield, talking to himself. "It's a Dodge truck, its black. It has a dented right front fender, the same as Kendrick's Chevy. It's about the same year. On a dark night, I don't think you could tell the difference between that truck and Kendrick's, especially if you was half drunk. Trenton, I want to do some more thinking on that truck I saw at the Barnes', go on in and tell Mama. I'll be back in a little while."

"Can I go?" I asked.

"Not this time."

"You think you should call Sammy?" I asked.

"No, not yet anyway. I'll be okay. Tell Mama where I am. Now go."

Sometimes it was hard being a kid. I wanted to help him but there was nothing I could do.

(42)

I told Mama what Daddy said and went to the barn to let Laddie out. He was staring at a haystack. I thought one of the pigs or chickens had got in the haystack, and then I saw the stack move and a boot sticking out.

Pigs don't wear boots.

The haystack burst open, and a tall blonde-headed, blue-eyed man raised up, hay falling away from his body. He saw me and froze. He was wearing striped coveralls with POW on his back. I started to run. Laddie ran under a table and growled at him.

"No, no, don't run away. I won't hurt you. Wait, please," he pleaded in an accent.

For some reason, I stopped dead in my tracks and looked back at him. "You talk American," I said, backing away.

"Yes, I need help," he said.

"You're a German. I remember seeing your kind when they came through town."

"I am an interpreter, a translator."

"What's an interrupter?"

"It's someone that speaks another language," he said. "Like now. I am speaking to you in English. I grow up in America. My father was a diplomat. He was called back to Germany when the war started. They sent me to the Army and my mother and father to work in the propaganda department of the Third Reich. None of us had a choice."

"Why did you come here?"

"I escaped. I had to. Another man ran and I was in the line of fire. The guards thought I was escaping, too, and were trying to shoot me. I ran until I was exhausted. I saw your barn and hid. They will kill me for sure if they find me."

"They won't kill you. They will take you back to the prison camp."

"No. They have orders to kill any escaped prisoners."

"What happened to the other German?"

"I do not know. We separated and he went one way and I another." I started backing up toward the door. "If I can get back they may not shoot me."

"They're not going to shoot you. We ain't Nazis."

"I am not a Nazi."

"You are too. You're a German."

"Yes, I am German, but I am not a Nazi. I do not belong to the Nazi party."

"What difference does that make, you're all killing Americans," I said.

"I have never killed anyone," he said.

"You never shot an American?"

"No, I am an interpreter, that's all I do. But they will shoot me anyway if they find me. There is a five hundred dollar reward for turning in a prisoner. I saw it on the bulletin board. If you could help me get back you would have lots of money."

"I don't believe that. You're trying to trick me."

"No, it is true. I swear."

"How am I supposed to do that?"

"Do you have a gun?"

"I'm not telling you anything."

"I do not want it. You can hold the gun on me, pretend you captured me, and get the reward."

"You think I'm stupid! You would say anything to get away."

"If that is true, why am I standing here? I could overpower you and make you reveal where your gun is. But I won't hurt you, I promise. I have to get back to the camp before they shoot me on sight. I was so scared, I took off running and ran and ran. I do not even know how far or which way the prison camp is."

"What's your name?" I asked him.

"Hans Victor."

"You're kidding."

"No, that is my name. What is your name?"

"Trenton O'Rourke," I said.

"I have some Irish ancestors," he said.

"Well you're not related to me."

"Help me, Trenton. If I can get back to the camp I may be able to survive. Germany is losing the war. It should be over soon. I want to be a doctor and help my people. I know they will need a lot of doctors after the war and that's the best way I can help".

"You're the enemy." I said.

"I won't let anyone know you helped me. They will think you are a hero for capturing me."

"My uncle was a hero. He killed a bunch of Germans, but they killed him."

"The war is a terrible thing for everyone," he said.

"How old are you?" I asked him.

"I am nineteen."

"We'll I'm ten. Do you think anyone would believe I captured you?"

"If you had a gun they would. That is an equalizer for anyone."

"How long you been loose?"

"Two days."

"You had anything to eat?

"No."

"My Daddy always said nothing should go hungry. There's sweet potatoes in that bin over there," I said and pointed to the bin.

"Thank you," he said and moved to the bin and picked up two sweet potatoes. "Can you eat them the way they are, or do you have to cook them?"

"You've never seen a sweet potato?"

"No."

"You can eat them like they are. They're real tasty." He bit down on the sweet potato and ate them both in record time.

"You were hungry. I hope I'm not doing anything wrong, giving you potatoes."

"You didn't give them to me. I took them."

"I'll call my daddy. He's a sheriff. He will know what to do."

"No, someone will find out and come after me. They won't care if they take me dead or alive. They just want the reward. I have to get back to the prison camp."

"Daddy won't shoot you unless you try to get away."

Laddie started barking at something I couldn't see. A few seconds later I heard hounds barking in the distance. It wasn't hunting season. "Did you come from that way?" I asked, as I pointed to the trees.

"Yes," he said.

"They have tracking hounds after you," I said. "They'll be here soon."

"I have to get out of here," he said.

"If you take that path," I said, pointing at the trail, "it will take you to an old house. No one lives there. There's an old pair of boots and overalls behind the barn door we use for cleaning the stalls that you can put on. There's a creek running through the trail with a hand bridge across it a little ways down the path. Throw your clothes and boots in the creek there and put the boots and overalls on, they'll wash downstream pretty quick. Maybe that will confuse the hounds and they might lose your scent."

"Get the gun and hold me prisoner like I said."

"That won't work. You better get if you don't want them to catch you."

"Are you going to tell them where I am?"

"I don't know. You better go."

Hans grabbed the old boots and overalls and ran out the barn door.

Laddie came out from under the table and sat down beside me.

I watched Hans until he was out of sight and walked back in the house, Laddie following along beside me.

(43)

The sound of the hounds barking got closer until I saw soldiers entering the barn with rifles.

Mama came out on the back porch, wondering what all the commotion was about.

"What are those soldiers doing in our barn?" she said.

"I don't know," I lied. For the first time ever I lied to my grandma. I believed what Hans told me and I knew if I told her she wouldn't see it that way.

A young soldier with captain bars on his collar walked up to the porch door and removed his helmet. "Ma'am, I'm Captain Edward Osman. We're looking for an escaped German prisoner. The hounds tracked him to your barn. You mind if we look in the house?"

"You don't think we're hiding him, do you?" Mama said.

"No ma'am. He may have snuck in."

"Okay, go ahead. Me and the boy will wait outside. Come Trenton," she said.

We walked outside and Laddie followed, rubbing up against my leg. One of the hounds came over and started sniffing him. He peed on himself. Maybe he wasn't going to be like Rin Tin Tin after all.

Captain Osman motioned for some soldiers to come in the house and they entered with guns drawn, carefully exploring every room. They were back outside in a few minutes.

"No sign of him in the house," Captain Osman said. "It looks like he was in the barn, though. I would stay in the house, ma'am, and lock the doors in case he comes back. He was wearing a POW uniform when he escaped but he may have different clothes now."

"Has he got a gun?" Mama asked.

"He didn't have one when he escaped but he may have now. Do you own a gun?"

"Yes, I got a double-barrel shotgun. If he shows up here he's a dead man."

"That's what I was going to suggest. Make sure your gun is loaded. If he tries to break in, shoot to kill."

"I intend to," Mama said.

"There were two but we had to shoot the other one. This one speaks perfect English. He's dangerous."

"I'll be on the lookout for him," Mama said.

"Make sure it's him before you shoot."

"I will," she said.

"Let's go!" the Captain yelled. The soldiers gathered and followed him into the woods, the hounds in tow, sniffing the ground.

"Let's go call Buzz," Mama said. "Get Laddie and come on in the house. I don't want you on the screened porch with this going on. You can bring Laddie in this one time."

"Yes ma'am. Laddie come here," I said but he didn't pay me any attention. He was too busy sniffing the ground where the hounds had peed.

"Laddie," I said again, louder. I got his attention and he came to me and we went into the house. I wondered what would happen to Hans.

Mama called the sheriff's office and Sammy answered. He said Daddy wasn't there. She told him about the escaped prisoner He said he knew, the Army had called him and he was organizing a posse to help them catch him. He also told us Norwell Tibbs and Ray Jones Sr. were coming to stay with us, and that Daddy was on his way home.

PART THREE
RIGHT THE FIRST TIME

(44)

Mama and I were in the kitchen when Daddy walked in and sat down at the kitchen table. He took off his hat and laid it on the table. "Sit down with me," he said. "I have something to tell you." We pulled chairs out and sat down beside him.

"We know about the German prisoner," I said.

"I know, and we'll let the Army take care of him," he said. "I just figured it out, we had the killer to start with. It's Ethan Barnes."

"You're sure, Buzz?" Mama said.

"Yes. The tire tread on Kendrick's truck matches the old Dodge truck Mr. Barnes owns. They have the same brand and size tires. It even has a dent on the right front fender. That's the truck Pete saw that night, not Kendrick's. Mr. Barnes said Ethan went to get fertilizer in the truck. But that was this afternoon and the truck's still missing. I think he's on the prowl for another victim. I have to find him before he finds one. Sammy said he told you Norwell Tibbs and Ray Jones Sr. are on the way here to stay with you until I get back. I have to find Ethan. Load your shotgun and lock the doors Mama."

"The soldiers were here looking for the German," Mama said.

"If I don't find Ethan soon he may kill again. I have to find him now. The truck is his cover. Let the Army worry about the POW. You and Tee stay in this house with the two best shots in the county to protect you."

"We'll be fine, Buzz, go," Mama said.

A car drove up with the two shooters. They walked up to the porch door and Daddy let them in.

"Make sure you take care of my family. I have to find Ethan Barnes."

"Don't you worry, Buzz," Ray said. "We will."

Daddy hugged me and Mama. "Lock the door when I leave," Daddy said.

"I have something important to tell you," I said.

"It will have to wait, son. I just don't have time."

"I need to tell you what happened in the barn."

"Later, I have to go." Daddy said.

He hugged me again and disappeared out the door.

Everything was happening at once. They were going to kill Hans, Ethan was a murderer, and Daddy could get killed. My whole world was crashing down at once.

We heard a noise outside and Mama got her shotgun. We looked out the kitchen window. It was the soldiers again. Captain Osman was coming to the door.

He knocked on the door and Mama opened it.

"Sorry to bother you again, ma'am, but the dogs lost the scent down the creek and we backtracked to start over. I don't know what he did but it threw the hounds off. They followed a scent downstream the creek a ways then lost it again. I was concerned he would come back to your place."

It worked! I thought.

"Excuse me for bothering you. It might be good if you and the boy went to a neighbor's house for a while."

"We'll be okay. My son is the sheriff. He appointed two deputies to stay with us until he returns."

"Good. We will probably have to kill him when we find him, but good riddance," Osman said.

They are going to kill him. It won't matter if he gives up or not. I have to get him out of there someway soon.

While I was worrying about Hans, Daddy was at Simpson's Feed and Seed trying to find Ethan. I later overheard him tell Mama what happened that day. Mr. Simpson was counting his receipts when Daddy walked in.

"Jerry, have you seen Ethan Barnes today?" he asked.

"Yeah why?"

"I need to find him."

"He might be down in river town, or down the road at the Green Frog. That's where he goes to get women now after that colored girl was killed. They're about the only ones that'll put up with him, but they wouldn't if he didn't give them a pocketful of money."

"Do you know the last time he came in to pick up fertilizer before today?"

"I can look it up. I put it on Mr. Barnes' bill and he pays me the first of every month. I keep a record of all his transactions."

"Would you do that please, it's important."

"Sure," he said and reached down under the counter, picked up a ledger book, laid it on the counter and started flipping through the pages.

"Here it is," he said. "July 27th. He picked up twenty 50-pound sacks of Nitrogen. I have his signature here."

"What time?"

Jerry looked down at the page. "Four thirty that afternoon," he said.

"Thanks, Jerry."

"What did he do? Run over something again?" Jerry said.

"I'll tell you later."

Daddy drove down to river town, looking for Ethan. The truck was nowhere to be found. He stopped at the High Time strip joint and went in. No one but Woody the owner was in the place. He was a big gray-haired, dark-skinned man with a history of arrests for minor crimes. He discovered he could make more money running his own strip joint than sharecropping. The white soldier boys weren't too particular about color when it came to partying.

"What brings you down here, Mr. Buzz? I know you don't drink and I ain't done nothin' to get arrested."

"I'm looking for Ethan Barnes, Woody. You see him?"

"Not today. He'll probably stop in later. He don't go to the Apollo anymore after that girl was killed. I got some new dancers comin' in tonight I told him about."

"If he does, don't tell him I'm looking for him, okay? Call the office."

"Yes sir, I'll do that."

"Thanks. Remember, don't tell him,"

Woody nodded.

Daddy told Mama he then drove back to Simpson's Feed and Seed and Mr. Simpson was getting in his car to go home. He saw Daddy and waited for him to pull up beside him.

"You need something else, Buzz?" he asked.

"One question. Did Ethan come in by himself when he picked up the fertilizer last month?"

"Come to think of it, he did. He usually brings a hand with him to load it but he didn't that time. My people had gone home and it was just me and him, reason I remember. I helped him load it. That's a little unusual. He doesn't like to work."

"Did he have anything else in the truck?" Daddy asked.

"Didn't notice anything else."

"Thanks, Jerry. I have to go."

"What's going on, Buzz?"

"Don't have time now, Jerry, later," he said.

Daddy said he drove away and began to put the puzzle pieces together in his head. Ethan knew his car would be recognized whenever he tried to dispose of the body. He drove back to the Barnes' barn, put the dead girl in the truck, and drove out to the Foster place and dumped her in the well sometime between midnight and daylight that morning. That's when Pete saw the truck. He was drunk and lost count of what time it was. His wife was probably furious he was late.

Daddy picked up the microphone and asked Sammy, "Have they found the German prisoner yet?"

"No, the posse hooked up with the Army and they're combing the county. I'm staying at the office, handling communications."

"Good, give Mama a call and check on her and my boy."

"You bet," Sammy said, "Don't worry, Ray and Norwell are there and your mama can shoot a shotgun better than any man I know."

"I'm looking for Ethan, I think he's the killer. Everything is pointing to him for sure this time. And there's a reason I need to find him now."

Everything was on a collision course.

(45)

It had been over two hours since the Army men were at the house. They would eventually get to the Foster place and Hans would be a goner. There was only one thing to do. I had to get Hans and hide him in our house until I could tell Daddy. That was the only way I could save his life. The trick was getting out of the house without being seen and getting back before anyone knew I was gone.

Ray Jones and Norwell Tibbs had parked themselves on the couch in the front room. Mama brought them each a jar of iced tea and they sipped the tea and smoked cigarettes. Both men were a picture of most of the other farmers in Angel Point. Sun brown, short hair, a straw hat, bandana around their neck, wearing overalls and work boots. Norwell had a Winchester and Ray a double-barrel 12-gauge shotgun like Mama's.

I devised me a plan. "Mama, I'm going to Daddy's room to listen to Sky King."

"Okay," she said. "Make sure the windows are locked and just go to bed in there. You can bring Laddie in."

I went to the back porch, got my radio, flashlight and Laddie. I stopped in the kitchen and scooped up a half pan of cornbread, filled a fruit jar with tea and went to Daddy's bedroom. I locked the door and turned the radio up loud. I wrote a quick note to Mama and laid it on the dresser. I wanted her to know I was okay if someone walked in the room.

I opened the window and picked up Laddie. "You got to go, too, big mouth. You would be barking your head off as soon as I was gone." I sat Laddie down outside the window, put the cornbread and tea in a pillow case and crawled out. I pushed the window back down.

It was a twenty minute walk in the dark. There was a full moon but it didn't help much. I couldn't turn the light on, it might attract attention. I had never made the trip at night. I hoped I could get there without breaking a leg. The soldiers could show up at any time and Mama would panic when she discovered I was gone. Laddie kept wanting to wander off in the dark and I never realized before how many sounds there were in the woods at night. Without knowing, I was the first to arrive. I walked up beside a window of the house.

"Hans, you in there? It's Trenton." No answer. I called again. "Hans, it's Trenton." This time, I saw one of the boards on the window move.

"In here, Trenton. Crawl through when I slide the board over."

I pushed Laddie inside and lifted my leg up on the windowsill and crawled in, holding the pillow case. I let the board slide back over the window and it was dark as sin inside. I turned on the flashlight. Laddie started growling at Hans.

"Hush, Laddie, he's a friend," I said.

"Am I glad to see you, Trenton. I didn't know which way to run. I heard the hounds coming and then the sound was gone."

"They picked up the scent of your clothes in the creek, but they lost it further downstream and came back to our house to start over. They will figure it out soon. I want you to come with me and hide in our house until I can tell my daddy and he'll take you back to the prison camp. I can't let them kill you for no reason other than you're a German. If it was in battle that's different. It's kind of like a catfish I caught once."

"A what?"

"Never mind. I brought you some cornbread and tea," I said and handed the pillowcase to him. He took the jar of tea and the cornbread out of the pillowcase and drank half the jar in one gulp. He sat the jar down and began to devour the cornbread.

"I was hungry," he said, poking the last bite of cornbread in his mouth. "Thank you for the food."

"You're welcome. I got to get you out of here before the hound's come."

"I can't let you do that, Trenton. You and your family could go to prison. That was a bad idea I had about you taking me prisoner. I was just frightened. You could be tried for treason, but there is something you can do for me."

"What's that," I said.

"I have a letter I wrote to my mom before I escaped. My family should know what happened to me. Would you take it to the Red Cross? They will send it to my family. The address is on the letter."

"Sure," I said. He handed me the letter and I put it in the front pocket of my overalls.

"You and the dog should go now," he said.

"What are you going to do?" I asked.

"The only thing I can do. Stay here, wait for them to come, surrender and hope they don't kill me. Please, go before they arrive."

"There's something I want to tell you before I go. My mother said I should find my dream. Because of you, I think

229

I have. You wanted to be a doctor. I think that's what I want to do."

"Tell the mother of the first baby boy you deliver to name him Hans," he said.

"I will," I said and we laughed.

"Best we stay here for daylight and we can see how to get to Vicksburg, Hans. I'll do what you asked me to do. I brought my rifle."

"If they see you holding a gun on me they may not shoot me," Hans said.

"Eat your cornbread and we'll get some rest. It's a long way to Vicksburg," I said.

As the night went by, we dozed and waited.

The sound of an engine woke us then stopped. Lights shot through the cracks in the boarded-up windows like silver swords being rammed into the dirty walls.

"They're here," he said. "Run, Trenton, before they see you."

"I'm staying with you," I said.

The lights went off. It was quiet again. We peeked out the window through the cracks in the boards. The moonlight was bright enough we could see outside. It wasn't the Army. A man got out of a truck and put a rope around a lady's neck wearing a colored halter and white shorts He started leading her to the Foster house.

"That's Ethan Barnes," I said. Ethan was close enough now to hear him. "Getty up, Shelly. I got you where I want you now, and you not goin' to get away from me 'til I say so."

"Take the rope off, Ethan, you're drunk," Shelly said. "I'm cold."

"I paid you to come out here. Don't give me no trouble or you'll wind up in the well."

"It was you?" Shelly said. "You murdered that girl."

"She had it coming," Ethan said. "The more money I gave her the more she wanted."

Shelly jerked the rope from her neck and took off running toward the road.

"Come back here, bitch," he said.

Shelly started yelling for help and running as fast as she could away from him. He pulled out a handgun and shot at her four times before she fell. He walked up to her, picked her up on his shoulder and started walking back to the house. He stepped up on the old rickety porch and dropped her. Then started twisting on the doorknob and pushing with his shoulder at the same time. The boards squeaked and cracked. Laddie started barking. I was trying to find my rifle in the dark.

"Who's in there?" he said. A light shot through the boards from his flashlight. Laddie was shaking his head, trying to get my hand off his mouth.

Hans picked up the rifle and moved to the wall beside the door.

The nails let go and the boards fell away from the door Ethan was pushing against. He stepped into the room with a flashlight and a revolver, leaving Shelly bleeding on the porch. Hans took a swing with the butt of the rifle against Ethan's head. He yelled in pain, dropped the flashlight and fell to his knees, still holding on to the revolver. Ethan shook his head, trying to get his wits about him. Hans took a step toward Ethan and pointed the rifle at him. Ethan turned on his knees and shot Hans. Hans dropped the rifle, grabbed his chest and fell backwards against the wall, sliding down to the floor. Laddie started barking at Ethan. Ethan picked up the flashlight and shined it on me.

"Trenton, what are you doing here?" he said. Before I could say anything Hans tried to get up. Ethan kneeled down beside him and placed the revolver against his head.

"Let Trenton go, please," Hans said.

"Who the hell are you," Ethan said, shining the flashlight in Hans' face.

"Hans Victor," he said.

"The German prisoner?"

"Yes."

"I heard about you escaping but I didn't know you could speak English."

"Please do not hurt him," Hans said and gasped for breath.

"Don't have a choice. Everyone would know what I did if I let you two live."

The sound of another car engine roared and lights covered the side of the house again, shining through the cracks. The car came to a stop. Ethan jumped up and looked out the window.

"It's your daddy, Trenton, but he won't do you any good. I'm going to kill you all."

I heard Daddy's voice on the car speaker. "I see the girl, I know you're in there, Ethan. Come out with your hands over your head."

Ethan looked at me and yelled back. "Not while I got your boy in here, Buzz."

There was silence for a few seconds. "Trenton, you in there?"

"Answer him," Ethan said.

"Yes," I said, as loud as I could. "The German prisoner, too. Ethan shot him, but he's still alive."

"Shut up, boy," Ethan said and pushed me away from the window. "Back off, Buzz! Move to the front of your car where I can see you and throw your gun away. If you don't, I'll kill your boy. You know I will."

"Come out and give up, Ethan," Daddy said. "There's no way out. Don't make it worse."

Ethan was looking out the window. Hans managed to get to his feet without Ethan noticing. He jumped at Ethan and grabbed the revolver. They fell to the floor, wrestling for the gun.

"Run, Trenton!" Hans yelled, hanging on to Ethan.

I jumped up and ran toward the open door, Laddie close behind.

Just as we cleared the door we heard a shot from inside the house. Daddy saw us running in the car lights and ran toward us. "Get on the ground, now!" he yelled.

I hit the ground and Daddy ran by me toward the house, his .38 in his hand with Laddie following. He stopped at the front door, took a quick look at Shelly, and went in.

A couple of minutes later he reappeared. "Come here," he said.

When I went in, Daddy had a flashlight on them. Ethan was lying face down on the floor in a pool of blood. Hans was on his back next to him, his chest covered in blood, still breathing.

"This is my daddy, we'll get you to a doctor," I said.

"It's too late," Hans said. "Remember to name the first baby Hans." He tried to smile but his lips would barely move. "Do not forget the letter."

"I promise," I said.

"You have a fine boy, Mr. O'Rourke," Hans said. He coughed, blood running out of his mouth, and closed his eyes.

"Don't die, Hans, don't die," I said and burst into tears.

"I'm afraid he's gone, son," Daddy said and put his arm around me.

Daddy picked up Ethan's revolver by the barrel. "Let's go, we'll get someone to take care of them." We walked out the door. "She's dead, too," he said, looking at Shelly.

We heard the hounds coming. Laddie ran up beside me and sat down by my leg. I opened the car door and he sat down on the back seat. We all got in and closed the doors.

"Looks like the trackers are coming. We'll wait for them," Daddy said.

A few minutes later, we saw lights flashing in the woods and the sound of the hounds got louder.

Daddy started up the car and turned the spotlight on the fender so they could see the Sheriff sign on the door. We saw the soldiers clear the wood line and the hounds sniffing the ground. Daddy turned on the loud speaker.

"This is Sheriff O'Rourke," he said. "There's a dead girl on the porch. Ethan Barnes killed her. He's dead in the house with your prisoner. He was shot in a fight to save my boy. I'm getting out of the car to confirm what I said. Don't shoot."

Daddy eased out of the car, keeping his hand away from the .38, and waited for the soldiers to reach him. Everyone was getting jumpy. Any sudden moves might trigger a bloodbath. The soldiers were a little trigger happy, anyway. It was like we were in a war zone.

(46)

As the soldiers moved in, I saw Captain Osman in the lead. He walked up to the car and the soldiers surrounded it.

"We'll check it out, Sheriff," Osman said.

Osman turned away and motioned for three soldiers to come with him. We saw lights inside the house. They came out of the house and Captain Osman came over to Daddy.

"That's him all right. We'll take possession of the body and you can do whatever you need to with the other ones. We'll require a statement later on about what happened here."

Two men came out of the house carrying Hans' body and threw him on a blanket like a sack of potatoes and rolled him up in it before placing it on their shoulders. Hans' head rolled out of the end of the blanked and bounced up and down as the men carried him.

I jumped out of the car and ran to him. "Why are you treating him like that," I said. "He's not an animal."

"He is to us," one of the soldiers said. "He probably killed several of our boys."

"No he hasn't. He never killed anyone except that no-good Ethan to save our lives."

Daddy walked up beside me. "Get back in the car, Trenton, now," he said, angrily. "We'll discuss this later."

"How do you know that, boy?" Osman said, looking at me. "Were you hiding him?"

"I'll handle my boy, Captain. You take your men and prisoner and go. I still got a murderer and a dead woman to deal with. Get in the car, Trenton. I won't tell you again."

"The FBI may have some questions for the boy," Osman said.

"Not if I can help it," Daddy said.

Captain Osman stood there for a second and called out to his men. "Okay, men, let's move to the highway."

When I got in the car, Laddie reared up on the window and started barking at the hounds.

"Laddie, sit down and shut up." I pushed him down in the seat hard and gave him a slap on the butt. My anger for the way they were treating Hans was spilling over to my dog. I realized what was happening and patted Laddie. "Sorry fella," I said and pulled him over into my lap.

Daddy stood beside the car and waited for the soldiers to leave the area. He closed the house door and got back into the car and picked up the microphone. "Sammy you there?"

The microphone crackled. "This is Sammy," he said.

"We got Ethan. He's dead and he killed Shelly. Send the coroner out to pick them up at the Foster place. I'll wait for him. Don't tell anyone about Ethan yet. Call my mama, tell her me and Tee are okay. That's all, nothing else."

"Your Mama discovered Trenton was missing about thirty minutes ago and called me. I tried to get in touch with you but didn't get an answer."

"I was kind of busy."

"You kill Ethan?" Sammy said.

"No, I'll explain when I get there, don't tell anyone about Ethan yet, you hear me Sammy?"

"Yeah, I hear you," he said.

Daddy hung the microphone back on the hook and looked at me in the rearview mirror. "You got a lot of explaining to do, young man."

"I had to try and save Hans," I said.

"No you didn't. You may not have realized it, but you were hiding him at the Foster place and didn't tell anyone, like the Captain said."

"I tried to tell you, but you didn't have time to listen. They were going to kill him whether he gave up or not. Hans was a translator. He never killed anyone before Ethan, and Ethan needed killing."

"That's what he told you and you believed it. Let's let it cool off a bit. I'm too upset with you right now to deal with it properly."

"Yes sir," I said.

Thirty minutes later, after the coroner picked up Ethan and Shelly, we headed to town. We saw Mr. Barnes' Packard sitting in front of the sheriff's office. When we went in, he was sitting on one of the straight-back chairs, wringing his hands. His sweaty, worn straw hat was lying on another chair beside him. He stood up and looked at Daddy.

"I heard there was some shooting at the Foster place. Did you kill my boy?" he asked.

"No, I didn't," Daddy said. "Ethan and the escaped German prisoner wound up at the Foster place at the same time. They both shot each other dead."

"Why did you let him kill my boy, Buzz?"

"There was nothing I could do."

Mr. Barnes' legs buckled and he staggered back to the chair and sat down. "Where is Ethan?" he asked.

"They took him to the morgue in Vicksburg. You can claim him after the coroner releases the body. I'm sorry, Mr. Barnes, but I'm glad we found him. He murdered another young woman. I suggest you go home and make whatever arrangements you need. We have to keep the truck a while for evidence. I'll let you know when you can have it back."

"I don't want it back. Take it to the wrecking yard when you get through with it. I knew something wasn't right when Ethan kept covering that truck up, but I wouldn't let myself think it could be something like this. I don't know how to deal with it," he said. He picked up his straw hat and shuffled out the door like he was forcing his legs to work.

When word got out about Ethan there was relief and anger. The Barnes family made plans to have Ethan buried in the family plot, but most of the townspeople were opposed to having him buried in the town cemetery. A large group of people organized a convoy and blocked the cemetery gate to prevent the hearse from taking Ethan to the graveyard, saying they didn't care if it had been colored or white, he was a murderer and shouldn't be buried in the cemetery.

There was no law or ordinance to prevent the burial, but the Barnes decided they would cremate the body like Sorenson to prevent vandals from digging up the body. The good people of Angel Point didn't care much about anyone's rights, they just didn't want to be buried in the same place as a murderer. Shelly's family had to take her to the white cemetery in Vicksburg to be buried. Cindila Williams had been buried in the colored graveyard a month ago.

(47)

It was time for Daddy to make a decision on running for Sherriff or going to work for Aunt Sara Beth. He said his hand was sore from all the congratulations for solving the case. The mayor had also approved a small raise. It looked like he wouldn't have any trouble winning, no matter who ran against him. When I asked him what he was going to do, he said he hadn't made up his mind. He said he was going to have another talk with Aunt Sara Beth and wanted me and Mama there.

The next day, we rode to town with him and went to Aunt Sara Beth's house. An older lady answered the door with a black bow in her gray hair, wearing a black dress and a white apron with lace around the edges. I wondered if Mama would wear that apron - probably not, too fancy.

The lady escorted us to the parlor. "Madam will be with you shortly," she said and left the room. There was a big stone fireplace like the Barnes' and I could feel the cold air blowing from the vents in the ceiling. This made two air conditioned houses I had been in.

We sat down and waited a few minutes before Aunt Sara Beth came in. She was wearing all her jewelry as usual, but she had on white silk pants and a frilly blood red blouse and black high heel shoes. Mama didn't say anything but I knew she didn't approve of women wearing pants. When she saw a woman in pants she would say, "If you're a man you wear men's clothes, but if you're a woman you don't."

"Would anyone like something to drink," she asked. We all said no.

Daddy shifted his hat from his right hand to his left and began to fidget.

"Sara Beth," he said, and swallowed hard. "I have given your offer a lot of thought. I sincerely appreciate the offer but I think I'm going to have to say no."

Me and Mama looked at each other and smiled.

"It's not because I think I would have trouble working for you," he said. "But because I need to find my own way. Please don't be offended, but I don't want you to pay for Trenton's education either. I have to do that. That's my job and I will find a way. I'm sorry we haven't been more of a family to you. You're welcome at our house anytime."

Aunt Sara Beth nodded her head up and down and looked at Daddy. "Buzz, I expected that answer. You're a proud man and I understand that. I respect it. If you change your mind or need help the offer is still good. Mrs. O'Rourke, Tee, I want you to know that you are both welcome at my house, too."

I was glad Daddy didn't take the job. I liked her much more now. Especially since Daddy wasn't going to be working for her.

It took a long time, but the wounds inflicted by Daddy and Aunt Sara Beth on each other had healed. I think that would have made my mother happy. I know it did me.

That happiness may be short-lived, though, because I was still waiting for the other shoe to drop on my punishment for helping Hans.

It was almost two weeks after Ethan and Hans died, Daddy was still mulling over what I did. He said he was caught between being thankful I was alive, thanks to Hans, and whipping the daylights out of me. He didn't know about the letter. I kept it in my pocket, waiting for the right time to give it to the Red Cross. I was tempted to read it but I couldn't read German. Hans' family should be the only ones to read it, anyway. I wanted to know what happened to Hans' body but the time wasn't right to ask.

That afternoon, Daddy called and said he was coming home early because an FBI man was coming to the house to talk to us about Hans. Mama hurried around the living room, putting everything in place and mopping the floor.

It was less than an hour after he got home that a black Chevy sedan with U.S. Government license plates came barreling down the road, stirring up dust, and stopped in front of the house.

A man stepped out wearing a dark suit and a felt hat. He was about Daddy's age, a little smaller, with dark brown eyes.

Daddy met him at the door and said for him to come in. He took off his hat, walked in, and Mama invited him to sit down and asked if he would like something to drink. He shook his head no and ran his hand through his thin brown hair and sat down on a chair and placed his hat on his lap. We sat down on the couch.

"Sheriff, my name's Robert Marvin. I'm a special investigator for the FBI. I have been assigned the task of interviewing you and your boy for a report on Hans Victor." He took a note pad out of his coat pocket with a writing pen stuck in the back and looked at me. "You must be Trenton," he said.

"Yes sir," I said.

"And you're Trenton's grandmother?" he said, looking at Mama.

"Yes sir," she said.

"Are you all American-born citizens?"

241

"I was born in Ireland," Mama said, "but I been here since I was thirteen."

"Ma'am, have you or any of your family ever belonged to the Nazi party?" he asked.

"What kind of question is that! Of course not," Daddy said.

"Hans didn't belong to the Nazi party either," I said.

"How do you know that, Trenton?" Mr. Marvin said.

"He told me," I said.

"I see. I read the Army report, Sheriff, and I understand your boy may have been hiding Hans Victor. Is that right?"

"Mr. Marvin, my boy didn't hide the man. He sent him to what he thought was a safe place until he could get in touch with me to take him back to Vicksburg. He overheard the soldiers talking about killing him. I was too busy chasing a killer to know it at the time."

"Sheriff, what he did could be considered treason, helping and harboring the enemy."

"Mr. Marvin, I was very angry when I discovered what he did, but I never considered it anything but a bad decision of a ten-year-old boy who doesn't know about treason and those kinds of things. If he had not sent Hans to the Foster place things could have been even worse. Hans could have run away, but he sacrificed his life to save my boy and he put down a serial killer. I would say Trenton was a very good judge of character, no matter what army Hans Victor was in. If we need to get a lawyer we will. To stray from the subject a bit, I requested help from the FBI to find a killer and was told with the war on it would be six months before they could consider sending someone to help. It's been less than two weeks since the incident with Hans and here you are to place blame on a ten year old boy There's something wrong with that picture."

"I get your point, Sheriff, but this is a turbulent time. Our world hangs in the balance. We have to check out anything that would undermine the war effort, no matter where it comes from."

Mama stood up, wiped her hands on her apron and gave Mr. Marvin a steely stare. "Sir, I lost a son in the war and I hate the Germans. Then, finding Trenton gone with an escaped German prisoner on the loose like to give me a heart attack. When I learned the full story I realized there's good and bad among us all, no matter where we come from. What's missing here is common sense."

Mr. Marvin shook his head and looked at me. "Trenton, I think you're a brave young man to do what you did, and I know where your Grandma is coming from. Sometimes we can't see the forest for the trees. I think I learned a valuable lesson today. There won't be any further questions. I'll submit a report and that will be the end of it. I'll go now," he said. He picked up his hat and stood up.

We all stood up. "Sir," I said. "Could I ask you a question?"

"Sure," he said.

"What happened to Hans? Did they send him back to Germany?"

"No, son, we can't do that. He was buried in an unmarked grave and his location and ID sent to Washington for future use if needed."

"You mean his family will never know what happened to him?"

"We don't have a choice the way things are now."

"Could the Red Cross get a letter to his family?" I asked. I was about to reach for the letter when he answered.

"It would probably never get there," he said. "I'm sorry."

"That's enough, Trenton," Daddy said. "Let it go."

"It's okay. I understand. I think the war will be over soon. Maybe you can get in touch with his family then."

Daddy reached a hand out and they shook hands. "Thank you, Mr. Marvin. I know you have a job to do. I appreciate what you did here."

"Sometimes it turns out good," he said, put his hat on, smiled and walked out.

After Mr. Marvin left, I hid Hans' letter in the barn and vowed I would get it to his family when the war was over. I owed him that at least.

(48)

The smell of bacon frying woke me. When I went in the kitchen, Daddy and Mama were eating breakfast. He had on his white shirt and dress pants and Mama had on her church dress.

"Are we going to church?" I asked.

"Yes," Daddy said. "Eat your breakfast and get dressed."

"You don't go to church," I said, staring at him.

"I do now," he said.

"He's not telling you the full story, Trenton. I heard him talking to Miss Paula this morning and he told her he would see her at church."

"I told her I was going, that's all," he said, looking a little embarrassed.

"After you learned she was going," Mama said.

"Mama, don't make something out of it. You're not supposed to eavesdrop on someone's conversation anyway."

"I won't go then," she said.

"You know that's not what I meant," he said.

"Than what did you mean?" Mama said.

245

"Okay, I would like to see her. That a crime? Besides, if I run for sheriff I need to be seen like Charlie used to, shake a few hands, that sort of thing. You satisfied now?"

"Not to mention you need to have a talk with the Lord to forgive you for not going to church," Mama said.

"That too."

"Get dressed, Trenton, so we won't be late," Mama said, and grinned.

When we got to church the new pastor was greeting everyone at the door. He was a slender-built man about six feet with gray hair and green eyes. His jaws dropped a little and his Adam's apple was touching the knot in his tie.

"Well hello, Sheriff, glad you could come," the pastor said, shaking Daddy's hand. "Mrs. O'Rourke, did you have a hand in this?"

"No she didn't, Reverend. I came because I wanted to come."

"Kind of," Mama said and walked past Daddy and went in. She found us a place on the second row and Daddy sat down beside Mrs. North on the row behind us. Mrs. Bailey and Melinda came in and sat down across the aisle from us. Melinda looked my way and I raised my arm up enough for her to see it and opened and closed my hand.

Aunt Sara Beth came in with all her finery on and sat down next to Mama. She waved at me so I waved back.

The pastor stepped up to the pulpit and asked everyone to sing Amazing Grace. As we were singing, I looked at Melinda and she was singing, too.

After church, Daddy was shaking hands with people. Mama was talking to Aunt Sara Beth and Melinda and her mother were standing by the driveway waiting for her grandpa.

I got brave, walked over to Melinda and said hi. She said hi and that was all. I didn't know if I should continue the conversation or disappear.

"Hello Trenton," Melinda's mother said. "You ready for school?"

"Yes, ma'am, I guess so."

Melinda was staring at me like she was trying to remember who I was then said "I found out we're going to be in the same room."

"Well that's good," I said. "We can help each other."

"Come, baby, let's go home," Mrs. Bailey said and led her toward her grandpa's car. Melinda looked back at me and waved. I waved back as she got in the car.

PART FOUR
LAST OF THE BEST

(49)

Mrs. Bailey called to ask if I could go to the picture show with her and Melinda. Daddy asked me if I wanted to go and I was speechless. Melinda wanted to go to the picture show with me, I couldn't believe it.

"Well you want to go, Tee?" Daddy asked.

"Yes, I'll go," I said.

Daddy let me out of the car at the Baileys' house. "Mrs. Bailey said the show's over at 2:30. I'll pick you up this afternoon around then," he said and drove away. I walked up to the door and knocked.

It became a regular thing for me and Melinda to go to the movies on Saturdays, with Laddie tagging along. He wasn't allowed in the theater, but they let him stay in the lobby and wait for us. I didn't realize at the time how smart he was.

I was only ten years old, but I knew I was in love.

I liked being with Melinda, but I was spending too much time away from Mama.

When I woke up the next morning I smelled biscuits, got dressed and went in the kitchen. Mama was taking the biscuits out of the stove. "Those biscuits smell good," I said.

"I thought it was time I made them for you since that's your favorite," she said. "Your Daddy went off without any but I think he's having breakfast at Melba's with that new school teacher. I heard him talking to her on the phone this morning, making plans. I think he's getting serious about her. You may have a new stepmom before long."

"That's okay with me," I said. "I like her."

"I do too," Mama said. "He's definitely sweet on her." We both laughed.

I sat down at the table. "You goin' to eat some biscuits with me?" I asked and reached for a biscuit, took a bite and gave Laddie a bite, too.

"Maybe later," she said. "I been thinking, Trenton. Maybe it is time to sell this farm. I don't think I'm up to working the fields anymore. How would you like to move to town?"

"Whatever you want to do is fine with me, Mama."

"We'll talk to Buzz when he comes home tonight. You need friends, and you sure ain't going to have any out here, except maybe that puppy. Maybe we could rent a place in town with plumbing and electricity and put the farm up for sale."

"You sure you want to sell the farm?" I asked her.

"Yep, I have been giving it some serious thought. Buzz is right. The day of the small famer is gone."

That didn't sound like her. She said a thousand times the only way she would leave the farm would be feet first.

"Since things are back to normal," she said, "why don't you go outside and play with Laddie, maybe walk down to the creek and show it to your puppy, and take your .22 in case of snakes."

I shook my head yes, finished off another biscuit and got up from the table. I started for the door when she called out.

"Trenton," she said.

"Yes ma'am," I said and turned back to look at her. She was leaning on a chair with both hands.

"You all right, Mama?" I asked.

"Sure. I love you, baby," she said.

"I love you, too," I said.

She smiled, sat down in the chair and took a deep breath. "Listen to your daddy, Trenton. He loves you, too. Take care of each other. You can do anything you set your mind to."

"Yes ma'am."

"Now run along and play with Laddie."

"You sure you're okay, Mama?"

"Yes, I'm fine. Now go."

"Yes ma'am," I said.

I went to the back porch and got my .22, picked up four .22 longs and walked down to Sugar Creek with Laddie, thinking about Mama and what had happened to all of us this summer. It didn't seem real.

I walked out on the log where I had seen the big catfish and sat down, looked downstream and thought of Beau, wondering if he ever got a puppy. Laddie decided to take a swim and jumped off the log into the creek and went under. When he came up he paddled like crazy to the bank, shook the water off and sat down on the bank and looked at me. I called for him to come out on the log but he sat on the bank whining. I saw a squirrel jump from a branch hanging across the creek to a tree on the other side. I picked up the .22 and loaded a shell. The squirrel was sitting in the fork of the tree, chewing on something. It was an easy shot. I aimed but I couldn't pull the trigger. I would be taking a life if I pulled that trigger, no matter how insignificant it might be. Those haunting eyes of the lady in the well appeared in my head. I didn't have the right to decide who or what lived or died by my hand.

An eerie feeling came over me and I got a chill in ninety-degree weather. It was time to go home.

I walked through the kitchen and into the hall. I didn't see Mama. Her door was open. I walked up to it and looked in. She was sitting in her rocker, her Bible on her lap with a marker in it. Her apron was folded, lying on the dresser. Her hair wasn't in a bun, it had fallen down around her waist. She looked like she was asleep. The only time she ever took her hair down was when the day was over and there was nothing left to do. I walked up to her. She wasn't breathing. I stood there looking at her. I wanted to cry but I couldn't. There was something about her that made me strong. I knew she wouldn't want me to cry. That's why she sent me to the creek. She didn't want me to be there when she died. I kissed her on the forehead, laid her Bible beside her apron on the dresser and the marker fell out. The marker was actually the deed to the farm she signed over to Daddy. I walked back out into the hall and picked up the phone and dialed the sheriff's office.

Daddy said she called him and said she wanted to sell the farm and had signed it over to him. He said he knew something wasn't right when she said she loved him. Her generation didn't say I love you very often - it was assumed, but not said.

Doc Crawford said her heart gave out. She had worked too hard for too long. We buried her next to Grandpa. Most of the town came except for the Barnes'. Daddy said Mr. Barnes thought it was better if they didn't attend since most of the people were still angry over what Ethan had done and they would only be a distraction.

We put her apron in the casket in case she needed to make a decision. I had lost my rock. She could face anything with strength and dignity, including her own death.

(50)

Daddy hired Mrs. Danton to stay with me while he was working. I kept seeing Mama walking around in the house. I don't believe in ghosts, but my imagination must have been working overtime because she was as clear as she had ever been, except when I went to touch her she wasn't there. Daddy said he saw her too.

We took Mama's advice and rented a place in town two blocks from the school. We bought the place the next year. I grew up there with indoor plumbing, electricity and a phone. As far as I know, Mama never showed up there.

After the war ended, I took Hans' letter to the post office and mailed it. Months later I received a letter in English, a thank you note from his sister. She said her mom and dad died in a concentration camp because they refused to work for the Nazis. They never knew what happened to Hans.

Cody Barnes came home and Mr. Barnes handed over everything to Cody for him to run. Cody bought our farm and turned it into a peach orchard and shipped peaches all over the U.S. Mama would have been happy the land was being used to farm. Mr. and Mrs. Barnes were very rarely seen anymore after Cody came home. When they died, everyone said it was from a broken heart because of Ethan.

Melinda's dad came home and went to work as a deputy with my dad.

As the years went by, I went off to college. I had to leave Laddie with my dad. My dad said he would go to the theater every Saturday. They would let him walk the aisles, looking for me, and he would leave and come back the next Saturday. Everyone got to know him and brought treats for him at the theater. I tried to spend as much time with him as I could when I was home. He knew all the tricks that Rin Tin Tin did and more. He really was my best friend. My dad said he disappeared one day and he thought he went off to die. The theater has been closed for years, but I still think about him every time I drive by.

I married the love of my life, Melinda. We had one daughter and we named her Elizabeth after my mother. Some folks tried to call her Liz but she insisted on being called Elizabeth. My Dad married Paula North and was elected and re-elected sheriff over the next thirty-four years. She helped him get his High School GED and he was more proud of that than being sheriff.

Paula replaced Blackstone as principle four years after they were married when it was discovered he misappropriated school funds, which was a nice way of saying he stole money from the school. He spent six months in jail and left Angel Point, never to be heard from again.

Daddy and Paula died two months apart in 1993. I buried them next to my mother, I knew she would understand why.

Aunt Sara Beth married a banker and got even richer. She kept the candy factory and paid for my college education in advance without Daddy knowing it, and refused to take the money back. Daddy borrowed the money from Sara Beth's husband's bank and put the money in her account. He was still paying on it when I got out of school and I paid it off.

Her step kids inherited the candy factory. It's still operating. There's always a bunch of kids outside waiting for the free samples.

The town never changed much. The wagon yard got turned into a bank parking lot. The stuffed figures of my grandpa and the others rotted away and they were never replaced. The old city hall building burned down while Blackstone was the mayor and they built a new one on property he sold the city. There's still a vacant lot where the old one once stood. The city council voted to keep Push but not to spend money to restore him. People still rubbed his deteriorating stone head for good luck. No one knows why.

Kind of funny sometimes, how certain memories stay with you. Another one, the dead lady in the well, I still see in my sleep every once in a while.

The sound of new people coming in the church for the funeral jarred me back to present day.

Three old men dressed in military uniforms that were too tight marched down the aisle and sat down. Beau's comrades from long ago had arrived.

I walked up to Beau's casket after the preacher was done and started to put his pocket knife in the casket before a thought occurred to me that it would be better to give it to little Trenton. I noticed someone had removed his pilot wings from his chest as I predicted. Boy, would he be mad. The honor guard removed Old Glory, folded it and handed the flag to Helen. That meant she was the closest one now. She walked up to me, leading Trenton, I watched as they wheeled his casket away.

"He loved to fly," I said.

"Yes he did," she said. "Alaska was the last place they would let him fly," she said. "He called it a puddle-jumping hunting job."

"You've been close to him then," I said.

"I have been. I noticed in his email you're a doctor with a clinic in Angel Point, Mississippi."

"My daughter Elizabeth and her husband David run it now. My wife Melinda and I retired two years ago, and we've spent most of our time spoiling great-grandkids. My grandson is president of a bank in Jackson, Mississippi. His wife's an attorney."

"Did you always want to be a doctor?" she said.

"I decided that not long after Beau left Angel Point. A man died saving my life and he wanted to be a doctor. It seemed the best way to repay him and do something useful with my life. I've never regretted it. Beau left the area before that happened. Your boy looks a lot like him when he was a kid."

I took Beau's old knife out of my pocket. "This was Beau's knife when he was ten years old Helen. He gave it to me then. I want to give it to your boy now, if that's okay with you."

"Go ahead," she said.

I handed him the knife.

His eyes got big as he reached for the knife. "Thank you," he said, rolling the tiger-striped-handled knife around in his hand, checking all its accessories.

"Grandpa would have liked that," she said.

"You knew him very well, didn't you?" I said.

"Yes I did."

"May I ask you a question before I go?"

"Sure," she said.

"I didn't hear Henry's name in the family funeral roll call. I wondered what happened to her."

Helen asked me to step away from the crowd and whispered to me. "We don't talk about Aunt Henry," she said. "My great-grandpa disowned her and said if anyone ever said her name again he would disown them, too."

"What did she do?" I asked.

"She became a civil rights marcher in California in the sixties and married a black man. My great-grandpa said she did it out of spite. We got word she died three years ago and they buried her out there."

"What did Beau think of that?" I said.

"He agreed with his daddy," she said. "None of us have ever seen her kids. We don't mix our blood in this family."

I was sorry I asked.

A sadness came over me. When we rediscovered each other, we always talked about the good memories and hid the bad. For that, we were both guilty of not facing the truth. I regretted it. It was time to go home.

The way we felt about each other as kids would not have been so as adults. The more I thought about it, the more I realized Beau and I had grown into very different men. He had embraced his father's beliefs without question, just as I had mine. I don't think we would have liked each other very much after that summer of 1944, let alone been close friends. It was different having chats on the internet. We mostly reminisced about our childhood and didn't talk much about our time as adults.

Before I boarded the flight home, I stopped off at a toy store and bought my great-grandkids a toy. Both toys had a limited lifespan with a warning that the sealed batteries could not be replaced; you threw the toys away and purchased new ones. My generation fixed things.

My father's generation is called the Greatest Generation. I agree, but all generations have made a contribution to history. Mine went to the moon, fought a long and controversial war, and finally recognized the true meaning of freedom for those who were free in name only. The next generation will write their epitaph, and then the next.

You're born. You live. And you die. It's what you do in between that counts.

A good man I would have never met had it not been for a horrible war made a difference in my life that would have never happened without that brief meeting. I always wondered what I would have become if Hans had not changed my life forever. Fate is an unknown factor in everyone's life.

The main thing I think about now, in the sunset of my life, is my loved ones and how the summer of 1944 changed the lives of everyone in Angel Point, Mississippi forever and that unforgettable Long Walk Home.

THE END

AFTERWORD

Everyone's life has a special time, people and place they never forget, and it instills memories that last a lifetime. They tell them to other folks to their last day, hoping some are carried on. I'm no different.

About the Author

John L. Lansdale was born and raised in East Texas. He is married to the love of his life Mary. They have four children. He is a retired Army reserve Psychological Operations Officer and a combat veteran with numerous medals and awards. Past roles include inventor, country music songwriter and performer, and television programmer. He produced and directed the Television Special "Ladies of Country Music." He has also produced several albums in Nashville, hosted his own radio shows and won awards for producing and writing radio and television commercials.

Lansdale was a writer and editor of a business newspaper. He has worked as a comic book writer for Tales from the Crypt, IDW, Grave Tales, Cemetery Dance and several more. He co-authored the Shadows West and Hell's Bounty novels with his brother Joe R. Lansdale. He is also the author of Zombie Gold, Horse of a Different Color, Slow Bullet, When the Night Bird Sings, Kissing the Devil, Broken Moon, The Last Good Day, Long Walk Home and several other titles.

TITLES from JOHN L. LANSDALE

SLOW BULLET

Army veteran Clark McKay is searching for the truth behind his best friend's murder. This search takes him across the globe, where he meets a multitude of characters and is forced to wade through the murky Washington DC waters of corruption. Clark McKay wants to find a murderer... but what happens when he uncovers so much more?

KISSING THE DEVIL

Young antiques dealer Megan Fields is gifted a beautiful medallion she doesn't want to take off...and can't, even when she tries! She begins to see strange visions and mysterious visitors. A dark evil is at work, and Megan's very soul is at stake.

BOY AND HOG

In the deep woods, anything can happen. A group of white-collar workers with a hand-drawn map trek into the wilderness for a hunting expedition. But out there, will they be the hunters or the prey?

BOY AND HOG RETURN

While on patrol, two game wardens stumble onto a grisly scene hidden deep in the woods. With backup on the way, will the wardens survive the wait, or will unexpected visitors send them to an early grave?

EMERGENCY CHRISTMAS

Join the Albright family and the guest who surprises them just in time for the holiday. Along the way, they discover sometimes crisis brings a family closer together.

THE MECANA FILES
by JOHN L. LANSDALE

HORSE OF A DIFFERENT COLOR – Mecana Files #1

Dallas PD Detective Thomas Mecana is on the hunt for a serial killer terrorizing the Lone Star State. Joining him is Darcie Connors, a young officer working her first murder case. With hard work, and some luck, Mecana and his partner discover a most-unusual serial killer case with murder in its very genes.

WHEN THE NIGHT BIRD SINGS – Mecana Files #2

Detectives Thomas Mecana and Darcie Connors are on the trail of a new suspect. With an ever-growing suspect list, Mecana must toe the line between friend and foe. Each action leaves them sitting in the crosshairs of danger. One wrong move could mean the end.

TWISTED JUSTICE – Mecana Files #3

Dallas Homicide Detective Sunday Verves is looking into the suspicious deaths of local drug runners when she discovers a potential suspect that hits too close to home. When the trail leads her south of the border, she enlists some old friends to track down the suspects.

THE BOX – Mecana Files #4

Just when he thought he was out...Thomas Mecana discovers a new killer has stolen old evidence from a case thought long-closed. When the bodies begin to pile up, Mecana knows he must take action. Together with a little help from his friends, they just might be able to stop a copycat murderer. This thrilling story brings Mecana face-to-face with pure evil.

STAY CONNECTED
WITH BOOKVOICE
AND
JOHN L. LANSDALE

Follow us online at
www.bookvoicepublishing.com
www.goodreads.com/johnllansdale

To contact the author for quotes, reviews, speaking engagements
or more, email John at bookvoicepublishing@gmail.com.